Welcome to The Beauty of a Time Limit!
A message from our sponsor:

Final warning! This story isn't for the faint of heart, okay?

Pfft, *faint of heart?* You call yourself a gatekeeper with that warning?

To be fair, we should always take precaution on what we consume.

W-Warning? Am I going to get in trouble?

Heh, kids like you shouldn't be near this area of the void…

What the heck are you yapping about? Are you really scared of people with masks?

No she's right… I can see various 'fun' events in the near future…

More information can be found at:
www.anotherchancestudios.com

The Beauty of a Time Limit

Edward I. Labarca

THE BEAUTY OF A TIME LIMIT

Copyright © 2020 by Edward I. Labarca

The following document is a work of fiction. Any names, characters, places, organizations, events, and incidents are the product of the author's creative thoughts or are used fictitiously. Any resemblance to persons, living or dead, events or locales is absolutely coincidental.

For more information contact:

Edward I. Labarca

labarcakvge@gmail.com

Library of Congress Control Number: 2020920898

ISBN-13: 978-1-7357082-2-5 (pbk)

Second edition

10 9 8 7 6 5 4 3 2

Dear dedications...

To the King that is Marcel Guimarães:

My Greenboy, your constant constructive support, persistent eagerness to see me grow and endless friendship helped me gather an immense amount of motivation to complete the story that was once never going to reach the light of day. I must thank you for being with me from the start of this adventure. I know I ramble a ton due to sheer excitement, but that's all because of you were there for me when no one was – without you, this would've literally never been possible!

To Ivisita's and her relentlessness:

Thank you for the selfless sacrifices you've done for your family, your own future, and for being the world's greatest mother. I am in debt to your endless kindness, positive outlook, constant support, and vision to create a world-changing event. Whether it is the heartwarming tender moments we shared or the days we reach our goals, you will always motivate me to move forward – This story is dedicated to those hardships we've overcome!

To Blake Spencer Osman and Jason Boyd:

Florida friends for four hours, forever! You have absolutely no idea how much I needed to see both of you. That short but intense conversation we had was just enough to prevent me from shutting down the entire project. This one goes to your endless sparking, friends.

To the reader – that's YOU:

You're a friend – for real. Thank you from the bottom of my heart – for your support, any potential feedback, and eagerness to read this story. Because of your interests and decision to read this very page, I will always be in debt for taking your time! I can't wait for you to see what's next!

Environmental Statement:

I also acknowledge that paperback books require physical paper, processing, and other factors that leave a large carbon footprint. I have made a pledge to plant trees per certain number of units that are produced. Let's keep it green for our wonderful world! A digital version of Time Limit has been published as well in efforts to combat deforestation, leaving large carbon footprints, and prevent any potential harm to our physical world. Please consider promoting sustainability!

Table of Contents

Formalities

Author Statement

Where to hunt down the Author   Like, the very first page of this book!

Official Title   It's on the cover, can't miss it.

Copyright Statement   Something like two pages ago.

Dear Dedications   On your left, buddy!

Table of Contents

The tale of the Unwinding Astra   Eh? You're currently here!

Bonus Content   Next page, okay?

The Beauty of a Time Limit

Act II – Consequences of Falsified Hope

Act III – The Crowning Revelations

Bonus Content!

Robot Recordings and Announcements

After death,
you've been elected to be reborn...
Congratulations and welcome
to the afterlife...

Compete for eternity —
or return to your *eternal slumber.*

Failure to protect the scarf that ties you into this reality shall result in *irreversible* consequences.

Unfortunately, *time is ticking...*
The Astral appendages that enable life are mysteriously fading away...

Will your fate end in *eternal happiness* or *permanent misery?*

Last one wearing the *champion's scarf* will be granted *another chance at happiness.*

"*...In this lonesome void,*

you may win your utmost desires if you wager

the possibility of losing everything you'll ever have.

You only get one chance.

Fortunately, you have nothing to lose...

You are made up of nothing, after all.

Will you make this run your best attempt?

Or will you be amongst those who have fallen?

Remember...

Death is promised.

Eternity is but a probability for you in this competition.

Will you take your chances and risk it all?

Will you win another chance at happiness?

Use everything you got,

For as this is the last strike...

Now wake up and seek happiness...

Only you carry the ability to attain your desired results."

— *The voice that the global graveyard once heard.*

Prologue:
The Explosive Hatchening

No one cares when no one is there...

It all started with a large, shattering crack that suddenly appeared in the gentle skies of the festive island of Imporia. The average islander quickly blames the perilous phenomenon at global warming – not for its disastrous threat in additive heat and irreversible climate changes, but because the island itself has always been rumored to be a living, breathing shell at rest.

Regardless of the fable where islanders inhabit on the surface of a hibernating beast's eggshell for eons, the growing concern on stopping this eerie sky-crack anxiously cripples islanders. What could they possibly do to prevent this ominous crack from expanding? Solutions felt impossible...

Time impatiently passes by and without warning, the island of Imporia abruptly explodes into trillions of pieces. The soft skies shatter into a dark void, depleting all visible light. Simply put; all life on the island had simply been eradicated without warning.

It was at this moment where, in the everlasting dark void, an unexplainable set of appendages spiral into existence. Bright, lavish and reflecting primary colors, this star-shaped ribbon vibrates and transforms the entire dark void into a blinding space of emptiness...

With the birth of the six-stranded star composed of cloth-like materials, the erased island spawns numerous amounts of undead islanders. With the celestial body silently floating over the empty void, it begins to gaze over all of the islanders once more...

And thus, the Astral Election begins.

In this empty canvas deprived of logic, a pair of trembling siblings gawk at the emptiness. What was once densely decorated with festivity and colors now haunts any remaining survivors... No sound, no skies, no life. Sinking into this unexplainable hollow world with no sense of direction mortifyingly haunts the lost duo.

The pair consisted of a fluffy-haired young boy who strongly held a doll with an over-sized button as an eye. Shuddering with the boy was his significantly older sister who could easily be mistaken as the child's legal guardian. Paralyzed in fear, the young boy tucks his bushy hair into this sister's severely scratched-up stomach.

The fear induced lady grows pale in this discomforting awakening. She sporadically looks at her environment to find absolutely nothing in sight. This lost limbo makes her want to panic, but her younger brother enforces her to display some level of courage. Upon further analysis, an older man distantly lays on the blank floor.

Locking eyes onto the grounded man sent the lady's heart spiraling further down her chest. In anguish, she continues to tightly embrace the boy.

Said man weakly lifts himself up. His quivering knees and flustered face were not a welcoming sight. "…What in darnation?" the man loudly complains to himself. His eyes were barely open and his skin was visibly feverish. "Where's the party at?" the man erupts again. The troubled man was clearly dizzy given that he couldn't walk properly.

Once the drunken senior gets a glance at the trembling siblings, he repeats his question more aggressively, "I s-said, where's the party at, huh?" the senior slurs, taking unbalanced footsteps towards the siblings. "*Reza*, I'm scared!" the boy sheepishly admits.

Despite her saturating fears, she does not hesitate to hide her younger brother behind her. The approaching drunkard raises a fist in the air. "A-Answer me!" he hiccups.

Out of impulse, Reza then shoves the drunkard, who easily collapses. The senior thuds and screeches about the aches he felt. "S-Snap out of it!" Reza shouts at the half-conscious miserable senior. "You're supposed to be the adult in the room, you drunk!" Reza shouts. She bends over to ensure that the drunkard could hear her hostility. Still aloof, Reza notices how the aching man was sweating.

She releases a 'tsk' and begins to shuffle her hands on the elder's collar. "You got to be kidding me…" she intensely says to herself. The young boy observes her swift hand movements. "You're sweaty *and* drunk! At least take off that stupid scarf…" Right when she unties the senior's red scarf, she swiftly pulls it out of his neck.

In the exact moment where the scarf was removed from his neck, the man begins to steam up. "Ah! W-Woah!" he wheezes in pain. His lips quickly grow crusty, his skin gets dry and steam overwhelms his body. "Huh!? What's going on?" Reza stutters at the flaring elder.

3

"H-Help! It burns! I can't feel—" the cries of the poor victim were interrupted by the overwhelming heat. In a flash, the man had evaporated from existence – as if he simply merged with the colorless void. All of the man's belonging evaporated with him; his clothing, his gear, his body. The only item left behind was the fabric that was yanked from him – a red scarf.

Numbed in disbelief, Reza shivers at the scarf that had held the man together. The young child drops its doll for he too couldn't comprehend what he had just witnessed. "*Amphy*..." Reza shakenly prompts, locking her eyes on the young child's yellow scarf. The stunned lady slowly gets on her knees.

Staring at the red scarf on her guilty hands, Reza could not stop violently shaking. "What are we going to do?" Amphy whimpers, tucking his head into his sister's dress. Trapped by the uncomprehendable accident Reza had performed, she felt her stomach churn in sickness.

What could she do? What must be done? What is going on? These thoughts aggressively ambushed her innocence. Reza gently latches onto her own scarf, then gulps.

"Amphy..." the soft voice of the guardian speaks. "We need to get out of here..." she motionlessly proposes. Reza slowly swoops towards the white floors to pick up the fallen doll. She gives it a careful glance before refocusing her attention to the scared boy. With a couple of tears glossing her royal violet eyes, she peacefully hands it over.

"Promise me that you're going to hold onto your scarf the same way you'd hold onto Mister Poo, okay?" her shaky yet tender voice commands. Amphy nods and Reza takes his free hand.

The two siblings begin to aimlessly roam the empty land of the void. Without any indication of anything or anyone, Reza was desperate enough to commit towards a singular direction.

Anywhere that led to protection.

Chapter I:
Hallways, Sympl and Mean

Welcome to the afterlife...

The devoided island of Imporia's existence only reminds its inhabitants about the forsaken clash of sudden disasters. While survivors wander the blank island's surface, one imprisoned victim fails to see the repercussions of the event. In a forgotten fissure, a grim garden prevails.

A murky tree that centers the abyss's soft floor perfectly statures near the victim's unconscious body. Its lack of leaves gave it a nude sense, yet it flourishes with glowing fruits that resembled a cross-fusion of apples and grapes. The breezy surrounding was covered by a few patches of colorless flowers and rakes of leaves piling over each other. Particularly, *Thevenin's* inanimate body silently rests over the soundless garden.

He was not alone, however. A compilation of darting clicks grew louder. The same noise began to produce weak buzzing and spurs of sizzles. It was revealed that a box-like robot had waddled near the unconscious body of Thevenin. The autonomous yet damaged box quietly debates with itself as it analyzes the floored Imporian.

It decides to conjoin its loose cables and slap his carcass. The slamming whip electrocutes the Imporian, waking him instantaneously. Thevenin jumps with a shriek. "H-HUH!?" the electrified man spouts. With his eyes finally wide open, the shocked Imporian gets to soak in the beauty of the abandoned garden.

On all fours, he scans the colorless petals and rich tree. He shoots his head upwards to see the white skies faintly shining. It was at this moment that Thevenin realizes that he was trapped in the bottom of the sinkhole he had fallen into. "Good mornteninoon." the robot beeps electronically. Thevenin's unfocused scanning is redirected towards the beeping voice.

"What the...?" Thevenin surprisingly mumbles. He observes the broken robot that produced steam. It clearly had its cables and wiring disordered, yet its main body looked intact. "What... What are you?" Thevenin questions in awe. The ripped machine continues to silently gaze at the confused Imporian.

"This unit does not have enough battery to continue operating autonomously." the malfunctioning electronic voice speaks. It's glitchy voice box made Thevenin spike up his posture. "Battery?" The robot then wobbles and continues to drag its slanted cables. It stops to slowly lower its body. "What are you—" the curious Imporian's sloppy wording abruptly comes to a halt. Without warning, the robot springs into the air, then relentlessly launches its searing cables at Thevenin.

6

Instead of directly shocking the Imporian, it wraps its slender cables around Thevenin's chest. "H-Hold on, little fella!" he shouts fearfully. Startled by the impressive jump, the hot cables began to compress against his chest. Now warmly hugging Thevenin, the robot blurts more beeping noises in a deranged order. "This unit will be recycling the voltage within you."

"Woah wait, are you like a vampire or something?" Thevenin frantically questions. His tied arms made him struggle to break free from the robot's vice grip. Not only that, but the robot's fumes were hissing all over his face. "Searching my internal dictionary for the term 'vampire.' Loading..." replies the glitchy robot. "No, I mean, like, are you trying to suck my blood for your battery or something?" Thevenin asks even more disturbed than before.

"Infraction of the first law of robotics: A robot may not injure—" the electronic voice gets interrupted by Thevenin's overwhelming wedge-in. "Hey, okay, keep it simple! Just tell me what you want and I can help you!" he erupts. The robot then pauses for a silent moment.

"...In critical response mode, this unit overrides permission. This unit has induced the target with a powerful shock. Assuming that the target operates a standard deployable body, the body may provide as a current to recycle the voltage." the robot speeches. Thevenin was too focused on stirring his head away from bursts of fried circuits and fumes. "Uh, can you like, not blow up on me, please?" Thevenin shakenly requests.

Submissive enough to obey his requests, the robot's body slides around Thevenin. It ultimately perches itself on his back, giving it an appearance of a backpack.

Amazed on how smooth it cycled around the gripped body, Thevenin simply gawks at it. "Battery stabilized. This unit will now begin the recharge process." the embracing robot states. Still, in a state of amazement, the Imporian catches himself hunching. "...Uh, does that mean you can let go of me now?" Thevenin asks gently.

"Negative. If this unit releases the body, the unit may not be able to operate properly." – "No, uh, you can do your thingy, but can you like wrap your tentacles somewhere else? You're squeezing me really badly, bud." The two reach an agreement when the burdening robot rearranges its wrapping position in order to mend itself.

The contracting cables were now hooked over the Imporian's shoulder pads. "This unit is thankful for your generosity. Critical response mode deactivated." it beeps weakly. Still baffled by the intelligence of the autonomous machine, Thevenin prepares a load of questions to ask. However, it's dying voice box makes Thevenin concern to what will happen to it.

Hey, did you wake me up? Where are we?

Error detected! Location unidentified.

An error...? Okay, how about the day? No, time! Do you know that? What time is it?

Time identified as stabilized 'Mornteninoon.'

Mornteninoon? You're as lost as I am, huh?

Repeating last statement: Location unidentified.

Right, duh... Sorry...

None of these responses enriched Thevenin's knowledge of his immediate environment. Lost in an unidentified sinkhole with a machine attached to this body makes him wonder what had happened during his slumber. In these thoughts, Thevenin begins to think more personally.

"...Well, do you have a name?" the inquisitive Imporian asks. "This unit does not have a 'name.' Overwrite 'this unit' with another label?" the robot replies flinchingly. Thevenin smiles on the opportunity of naming his new companion. "I'll call you simple."

"Affirmative. To confirm, please spell out the name." the robot faintly demands. Thevenin jokingly scoffs at this, "Pfft, easy. S-Y-M-P-L. Simple!" Upon granting his backpack the gift of a nickname, *Sympl* releases another blaring alarm.

"Rebooting process will shortly begin." Sympl announces. "Rebooting...?" Thevenin question in confusion. "In order to realign to my most optimal form, I will need to reboot my systems while using your body as context." The robot explains. His wording does not help the lost Imporian understand the situation. "It'll be painless." Sympl cynically adds.

"P-Painless?" Thevenin hesitates. "Trust me. I do not plan on harming your body." Sympl states. Tension in Thevenin's shoulders were physically felt by Sympl. "...At least I do not intend to." Sympl adds. The fear

9

induced Imporian continues to shudder. "A-Ahem, well, if this is part of the process, then I supposed it's okay." he reluctantly concludes.

"Fear not. Your body is very durable. It shouldn't take any damage with the reboot." Sympl triumphantly states. "Perhaps you can ease up a bit if you help me understand how you ended up in this hole?" Sympl bleeps as its body begins to cool down. "Huh?" Thevenin asks in confusion.

"You remember a world before this one, correct? Why don't you tell me a bedtime story before the reboot process kicks in?" Sympl questions. The confused Imporian tilts his head in confusion. He gently rubs his chin, "A bedtime story already? Robots go to sleep?" Thevenin speaks as he begins to recall the events that previously occurred.

"Well, it was an ordinary day in Imporia. I was just doing my job, and—" Thevenin's explanation gets interrupted as the robotic companion blares an eruptive beep. His heart skips a beat as he is not used to Sympl's unexpected alarms. "Job? What is that?" the perching robot questions.

"Uh, you don't know what a job is?" – "Negative." – "Well, it's a series of tasks you do in exchange for something." – "Does that mean that my job is to protect you in exchange for you to carry my voltage?" Sympl questions back as it continues to gather data from its host. "You could say that... However, I am a *gatekeeper*. Which means *I'm* the one that'll do all the protecting." Thevenin confidently replies.

"Gatekeeper?" – "Yeah, we go around the island and make sure everything is safe! If we see some weird activity, we will handle it!" Thevenin continues to speech to his friendly backpack.

"We..." Sympl quietly states. With its voice box's volume steadily decreasing, Thevenin continues to paint Imporia to Sympl. "Yeah, 'we' because there's a very small group of us..." Thevenin clarifies.

"Anyway, I saw a huge crack in the sky! I've never seen such a thing before! It looked like if the sky was going to fall apart or something." he continues to speech. "A crack in the sky?" Sympl questions once again. "Yeah, it was growing for a couple of days and before you knew it, everything just, well, exploded!" the talkative Imporian continues to explain.

"If the sky was cracking apart, why didn't you put tape over the crack?" Sympl questions. Thevenin pauses and ponders on the question. "Uh..." the Imporian mumbles. "You can't just tape the sky back to normal, Sympl." Thevenin murmurs, holding back a bit of laughter.

"But did you *try* to seal it?" Sympl barks. Once again, Thevenin shudders at Sympl's oddities. Its illogical explanation prevents the Imporian from thinking rationally. "Sympl, do you not know how the sky works...?" Thevenin goofily asks. The two remain silent as Sympl's body begins to muffle purring sounds.

"What are you doing?" Thevenin frantically questions. "Rebooting will begin shortly..." Sympl shoots back. "Oh, okay. So, to conclude, I was going to do my job and save people." – "How? You didn't have tape with you, did you?" – "No, I was going to gather islanders into the watchtower where I work at!" Thevenin remarks.

"Watchtower?" Sympl's voice gets weaker. "Yeah! I didn't tell you yet, but I guard Imporia's watchtower as a gatekeeper because it's like an indestructible tower. Even if the island blew up with earthquakes and floods, nothing could beat the watchtower!" Thevenin declares.

"Well, at least that was my plan until Zyra cut my leg!" Thevenin remorsefully announces. "Zyra...?" Sympl's voice almost reaches mute. "Oh right, she's another gatekeeper. Well at least isn't anymore. I don't know, my dude. She literally got in the way of saving people! Like, why would she do something that horrible? Isn't that what she signed up for?" Thevenin uneasily speaks to himself.

"So, there I was, paralyzed on the streets of Imporia. The sky exploded, I couldn't move, before you know it, I blanked out and then you woke me up." Thevenin monologues. Retracing the events that led him to the relatively grey sinkhole eases him a bit. However, his clear depiction on how he reached an odd circumstance felt farfetched to himself. "Look, I won't understand how this all came to be, but the point is, I'm here now. What about you? How did you end up in this ditch?" Thevenin questions.

"Sympl...?" he questions once more realizing that his clingy partner is essentially asleep. Tucked in after a fictional bedtime story, the robot produces a faint buzzing sound. Could the robotic companion have reached its promised offline state? Regardless, the Imporian exerts a sigh of confusion. "Hey, how long is your reboot?" he questions, failing to get any response. Thevenin notices that its searing cables begin to cool down. Even with Sympl holding onto Thevenin in a burdensome fashion, the cool-down fills the Imporian with relief.

Absolutely isolated in the deep sinkhole, with no possible activities to explore, Thevenin locks his gaze on the large tree planted in the center of the garden. Particularly, he begins to investigate the glowing contents on its dark branches. Awed by the vibrant reddish-magenta-colored orbs that trickling amongst the tree's dark branches, the Imporian catches a whiff of its juicy scents.

"...What is this place?" he questions to himself in silence.

Somewhere else...

In the blank skies of the void, the star-shaped ribbon's grey cloth wriggles violently. The grey appendage that once extended unworldly lengths had been shrinking for some time now. Due to its absolute minimization, it begins to coil the rest of its heavenly body into the shape of a petal. Without the flowy ribbon weakly dangling from the bright celestial body, a shift in the colorless island occurs.

This steady process emits a turbulent breeze throughout the entire devoided island. Followed by rushing winds and a loud but soft chime, its volume was loud enough for it to be heard by the heavens.

All surface-roaming survivors felt the cold blow exert its sudden force onto them. Mysteriously, some inhabitants phased into the colorless atmosphere without trace. Others remained completely unaffected. Followed by the ribbon's expiration was a puny shockwave that tickles the blank ground, leaving small trails of metallic bits.

One of these inhabitants that felt the gust of blustery wind flinches in agony. She was a lost gatekeeper of Imporia who carries the regrets of a thousand burning faces – *Zyra*. Completely isolated by herself in this infinitely empty plain, the anxious lady tightly grips onto the only precious gift she had left. Her means of defense and a reminder of a tender bond – an odd, stone-like sword.

She desperately searches for any sign of life. With the burst of wind fading away, she spots fragmented patches of colorful pebbles ahead of her. Thinking that her vision had tricked her, the gatekeeping guardian madly dashes at the new location.

As she approaches the structure, she finds an empty, abandoned arena. How could a structure of this magnitude survived the massive explosion?

Her pacing slows down at the entrance of a chiseled colosseum. The emptiness of the architecture haunts her. What was once a gathering for social events and celebrations now embodies the hollow feeling of the void. This arena... Was it not one of Imporia's famous spots for festive congregations? Or is her mind playing dirty tricks against herself? The ever-wrenching solitude lingers in the back of her mind.

Zyra squints her eyes at the abandoned colosseum hoping to find a sign of life. She opens her mouth, ready to yell out for someone, yet she hesitates on the idea of calling out strangers. Her search for life has been dragging long, but this particular place gave her an uneasy feeling.

She glances at the crumbling arches only to see a figure rattle away from her sight. Startled, she draws her blade and heftily prepares for anything. Her eyes continue to scan the empty arches for life only to be jumped by a voice from above. "...Oh, pardon me. Did I already offend you from all the way up here, fruitcake?"

Zyra shoots her head towards the highest point of the Colosseum to see a faceless man relaxing. The slim body cockily snaps his fingers, signaling a trigger of some sort. Perplexed, Zyra winces at the unidentifiable figure. The snap releases a stampede of other strangers with cloth covering their faces. During their fast-paced march, Zyra tries to keep up with the sheer amount of people that eventually surrounded around her. Coordinately, they border the armed guardian in just a few seconds.

Now tensed up, the gatekeeper quivers once the crowd reveals its sashes of weapons, gears, and matching blue scarfs. "**Aphotic**... We have an unexpected visitor." the voice from above spoke, hushing the crowd's murmuring. The sitting slender man rolls over and proceeds to dive down into the ground below.

The man swiftly lands, finally leveling himself with Zyra and making himself fully visible. He was faceless due to wearing a white plate as a mask which was held by a metallic wrap. Underneath the mask was a thin layer of wool that covered his entire head except for his mouth. He wore a torn, sleeveless tuxedo that covers his scratched-up button vest. His hat complimented his noir-fashion. However, his arms were drenched in a deep red color as if they were massive flesh wounds.

The defensive gatekeeper, speechless at the man's entrance, gawks at his bloody arms. "Is that how you wield a weapon? Try to hide the scared look in your eyes first..." the masked man observes. He approaches her fearlessly, only making Zyra clench her blade tighter. Ready to retaliate, the masked man breaches her personal space.

"It's all so familiar..." his revealing mouth smirks. "Could I place my finger on it...?" he adds unnervingly. The disheveled man backs away from Zyra confidently, crossing his red arms in the process. "Out of all the people who aimlessly wander here, it's a pure coincidence that you've made it." he comments with his back facing her blade.

The audience of similarly dressed personnel struck a feeling of stage fright towards Zyra. This reminds her that these weapon-wielding masked members were watching her every move. Being around public crowds was not only one of her fears, but she was aware that she could not commit to brash movements due to being outnumbered. This ultimately racks up her nerves and weakens her stance against the masked man. Clueless on what is going on, the masked man continues to speak.

"Can't believe you're in this comical predicament. We're trapped in this pointless husk and now we have a 'heroic guardian' from the watchtower?" The masked man then turns directly at her, "The best part is, you're not just any gatekeeper — You're a traitor. Yes... you ran away, didn't you?" he questions, tailoring his statement to the nosey crowd.

Sweat trickles down Zyra's neck upon hearing this. What little color was left in her pale face disappears. The crowd surrounding her begins to murmur and rustle against each other.

Insecure of responding, she reluctantly tilts her head around the crowd to see them talk amongst themselves. "...I see you're not denying it. Perhaps that's why you're alone? Well, that's just perfect for all of us..." the masked man cockily says.

The crowd begins to rumble louder. The masked man hushes the crowd with his strong voice, "Settle down, settle down... I thought gatekeepers were supposed to risk their lives for others." Petrified at how the masked man continues to utter nonsense, Zyra darts her eyes in an attempt to find an escape route.

The masked man continues to give his speech around his audience, giving the guardian a spotlight in the process. "In fact, a true gatekeeper of Imporia would've worked in a team and save countless victims, no? Instead, we're standing here right now, yearning for a desperate release." he huffs. "It seems that you have other ideas running in your mind, huh?" he deviously adds.

The blank-faced speaker releases a heavy sigh. "However, I'm thankful we're finally here in this void since I have unfinished business to do." The sinister crowd remains silent upon this announcement. Zyra transforms her fearful look to a sterner expression. With this, she grips her weapon as tightly as possible.

Too many questions flood Zyra's noisy head. What does this faceless man intend to do? What does he mean by unfinished business? More importantly, how can he pin-point Zyra's lonesome approach?

"...With that being said, fruitcake, I'm going to need your cooperation." the masked man announces, silencing the crowd behind him. Zyra takes a moment to analyze the stone-cold expression the masked man had exerted.

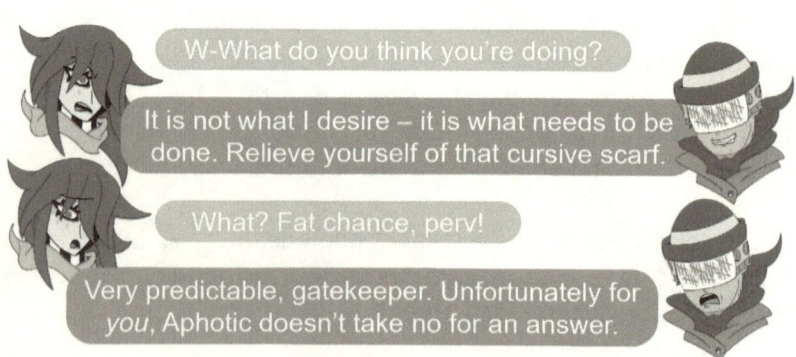

W-What do you think you're doing?

It is not what I desire – it is what needs to be done. Relieve yourself of that cursive scarf.

What? Fat chance, perv!

Very predictable, gatekeeper. Unfortunately for you, Aphotic doesn't take no for an answer.

She felt disgusted that the masked man had suggested to remove an article of clothing – especially in a crowd. In this critically tense time, she still couldn't manage to find an escape route, forcing her to awkwardly face the masked man. "I need you to understand that scarves are plaguing our existence." the leader speaks, now crossing his bloody arms. "We're trapped here, but I'm not letting us stay here forever. So, hand over your scarf already."

Zyra snaps, "Why do you want this useless piece of cloth so badly?" The crowd grows visibly stressed as the calm masked man aims his direction into the skies. "See that thing in the sky?" the masked man questions rhetorically. Zyra was hesitant to unlock her eyes from the menacing leader.

Out of curiosity, she uses her peripheral vision to see the floating ribbons. The leader continues to calmly lecture his legion. "A rather close associate of mine has indicated that it has a name. It's known as 'the Astra.' Most importantly, the colors of the ribbon dictate how relevant you are to the election." the masked man speeches.

"The election...?" Zyra immediately questions. Now amused at her question, the man begins to grit his teeth. "I don't know if you've noticed already, but none of us have a green scarf." Upon stating this, the crowd inches closer to Zyra. "And my organization needs to stay relevant to finish our business."

Zyra takes in the chilling glare of one hundred faceless strangers.

Chapter II:
Eerie Associations

In order to survive, you must seek eternal alliances...

Zapping and crashing, the two siblings were being chased down by a figure who wore wool to hide its face. Behind a broken wall, Reza tightly holds Amphy with all of her force. The hunter's footsteps grew louder and closer to the covered siblings.

Before the hunter could peak clocking at the hidden corner, a distant voice yells out, "Sir, please! What are you doing?" Evidently, the voice spurred from behind, making the hunter place his head over his shoulder. The masked hunter was greeted by an old man holding a cane.

The old man gives a gentle wince to the halted hunter. "Why do your people keep hunting others? Don't you understand that a scarf is what holds us together? Are you challenging that?" the elder frets. In this decisive moment, the hunter fearlessly faces the elder.

Still frozen in fear, Reza and Amphy continue to remain silent. The older sister gleams ahead of her to see more empty roads. As she calculates an escape route when suddenly, an explosive gunshot was heard. Both siblings flinch from the shot and even release tears from stress.

Racing in the mind of Reza were reminders of her hunching over Amphy. She trembles in real-time, yet she can't help feel how the void's shining environment replicates the dark depths of her youth.

The echoes of hostile footsteps resume, drawing ever so closer. "It's safe now, you can come out." a calm voice announces. Was the soft serenity of the elder voice safe? Or was the figure going to plant a foot onto Reza's torso and plummet her away to the depths of hell again? Nothing would procure Reza's decision to move on – her heart races in terror.

The possibilities uncontrollably force Reza to shackle herself onto Amphy. "Look, I know you're scared, but..." the firm voice pauses. Upon his sudden pause, the elderly voice had a clear sight of the sibling's bent heads.

"Please, there are no more threats. I'm in need of help." the elderly voice cries out again. Reza drags Amphy back into her chest, hushing his words by placing his mouth on her neck. Despite this, she could not retain herself slipping words of her own. "Not again... Not again..." she rocks in panic. Had the hunter been truly defeated or is he using the mockery of an older voice to lure them out?

"I know how scared you must be." the elderly voice spoke again. Without warning, the footsteps begin to draw nearby. Reza senses the silhouette of a monster drawing ever-closer to her. It only took a matter of seconds for the voice to reveal its figure.

The voice did not lie; an elder man with a cane assertively sways over the corner of where the siblings were hiding. Just like any other person in the vast void, he wore a reddish scarf that wrapped around his neck. He was hunching, yet tries to give a pacifist vibe. "Please, we're looking for a way to get out of this mess..." he pleas.

Reza's heart skips a beat seeing the man's face pop out of nowhere, yet she finally realizes that both the threat of the hunter and the figment of her trauma vanished. Not only did she get startled, but Amphy too squeals out his sister's name in horror. The two siblings were still shaking in fear but had settled to believe that the worst was over. As a result, they slightly calmed down upon being greeted by the older gentleman.

"Stay away from me you monster!" Reza snarls aggressively. The elder takes a step back at Reza's barking. He then gazes his eyes at the scared siblings, "Weaponless?" he whispers to himself. Reza stands up and jets herself towards the elder. She points at him, "You got a lot of nerve showing up all willy-nilly!" she spouts aggressively.

"Please calm down." the elder replies uselessly. Reza continues to near the elder's chest, "You think you can just tell us not to be scared? Not to fear for our lives?" Reza continues to cry out. The elder holds his hands up in an attempt to signal peace. "Look, we've been wearing the same shoes for a while now, young lady!" the elder responds.

"Same shoes!? How dare you think you can even imagine what I've gone through, huh!?" Reza hustles. "We're all stuck in this damn place. We've been looking for an exit since we got here and I think it's just better if we cooperate." the elder continues to speak. Still frowning, Reza tilts her head upon hearing his words. "*We*? There is no and will never be a 'we', old man!" she slurs before turning her back at him. The elder takes a deep breath after getting snapped by Reza.

"Fine. Go ahead. Leave right now. How will you defend yourself next time one of those hunters tries to take your scarf, huh? You didn't even attempt to move when you had a chance! Do you know what happens to those who are too scared to do anything?" the elder questions. Stubborn, Reza crosses her arms and pouts away from the elder. "...Mind ya' business, fool!" she yells in annoyance. Amphy begins to tug her arm, "Reza, what if this man is trying to protect us?"

The young boy's question made Reza snap yet again, "Protect us? Bah! There's no such thing as a protective adult, Amphy. It's just me and you." Her strict expression hushed the troubled child. To wrap up their conversation with the heroic stranger, the siblings begin to face the endless void once more. Full of anxiety, they hesitate to cross the abyss once more. "Please, don't go! I can't leave innocent children behind knowing that you're vulnerable to another one of those attacks." the elder insists.

"I'm not your responsibility, pops." Reza loudly declares. Her confident posture begins to crumble as soon as she hears a stampede of footsteps. Two more figures behind the elder revealed themselves. "Coast is clear, *Grant*. No sign of any hunters." A chubby figure announced.

"Very well... Children of the void, please. My team and I do not have the heart to hurt any innocent survivors. You need to know that there are a few of us and many of those foul-stench hunters." Grants states. "Our team can't let them collect scarfs like that! It'd only make everyone's situation worse..." Grant gloomily adds.

"Many of them? Make the situation worse? Team!?" Reza keens. Grant oddly takes a quiet step back. "The whole island eradicates itself and now you gotta' deal with people who have guns for no reason!? Scarves!? They want scarves for what!? How the hell did these scarves appear out of nowhere, huh!? I never even had a scarf in my closet! A-And you think I'm stupid enough to just help some old man, let alone let my guard down near one!? I am not going to deal with any of this today! Stay the hell away from me!" she rapidly blurts in anger. Both of the siblings then focus at the colorless horizons for a few moments before making any more brash movements. In silence, Reza careens her head back at the gentle elder.

Amphy gazes at his frustrated sister. "Are we going to be okay...?"

The hot-headed lady deflates her posture for a moment with an unsteady sigh. For what felt like a very long pause, she slowly opens her mouth. She then turns at the concerned elder, "I... I may be defenseless and scared out of my mind, but that won't stop me from protecting the only thing I have left." she begins to wager with tears trickling down her cheeks. "I don't care how many times I have to hide from those freaks... I just can't afford to lose him again." Reza anguishes in tension. She gazes at the young boy who desperately holds her hand.

"I remember having family too, y'know?" the elder weakly says with a sorrowful wince written all over his face. "Therefore, I can understand your pain, young lady—" the elder sympathizes before Reza snaps. "Stop comparing, fool..." More silence enrolls. With no real turbulence obstructing itself from the nearby team's investigation of the broken town, Reza once again speaks up.

"...What do you *really* want?" she queries with a cold, stern face. With all eyes on her, Grant responds with, "I firmly believe what needs to be done to escape this void. I need all the help I can get."

. . .

Simply put, an unknown amount of time passes by.

Sympl awakens to find Thevenin eating the last fruit of the tree. Curious to the body's activities, the robotic backpack runs a scan on itself to verify its conditions. It silently detects that its reboot was oddly interrupted. What prevented it from its completion? Self-analysis indicates there was a physical change that *did* occur – just not to Sympl's desires. Without any idea of its disruption, it begins to rely on the only person available to it.

"Good mornteninoon." the robotic voice blares, startling the gluttonous Imporian. "Sympl? You've been asleep for days!" Thevenin replies. He was joyful of the fact that he had someone, or rather, *something* to talk to. "Impossible. The reboot only took a few minutes."

Puzzled, Thevenin explains that Sympl's sense of time was absolutely wrong. Upon proving to him about the false sense of timing, Thevenin realizes that the sky hasn't darkened either. No nights have swung along with the skies. The outlook of the sinkhole's surface only shined a dim white shine. "No, *that's* impossible. You can't tell me it only took a few minutes to eat an entire tree. It had to take me at least a week!" Thevenin states.

"Eat an entire tree…?" – "Yeah, although I haven't felt a difference in being full or being hungry as a matter of fact…" Thevenin awkwardly replies. The robot then beams its visors back at Thevenin's direction to see that he had a completely different look.

For starters, his scarf had multiple, long flaps rather than a singular tied knot. It was stained a different color and covered Thevenin's chest like an apron. Thevenin's yellow skin grew toner, his lips were chapped, he had blank eyes and even grew sharp fin-like ears. Additionally, two large fangs erected out of the scarf.

Thevenin pauses for a moment and slides his hand under the flaps. The Imporian grew insight onto his scarf; the grey neckcloth was now magenta and six large flaps shot out of his neck. Shaken, Thevenin touches his ears to feel the straighten fin-like ears. Sporadically, he jumps around and catches a glimpse of flowing appendages while feeling odd textures on his deprived face.

What has he become?

"Sympl?" Thevenin yelps out. "What's going on?" Sympl's cables whip out and extend around the flaps of the scarf. With the rebooted version of Sympl, its cables recovered from its torn damage. Even its darting aglets were covered by a new coat of plastic. "I cannot detect if your voltage has caused the alteration. Perhaps you are allergic to the consumed content, Volt." Sympl suggests upon swiveling its cables around him.

"Come to think of it, I've never seen those fruits in my life before..." Thevenin comments. The Imporian calms down once he takes a minute to observe his new aesthetic. Between the excitement of hearing Sympl's voice again and the confusion of his body's corruption, Thevenin aimlessly stares at the surface.

"...Wait, what did you just call me?" Thevenin interludes. "Considering that you are circulating my entire electrical spirit within you, I've decided to nickname you Volt. That is unless you have another name I may label you as." Sympl robustly replies. Thevenin chuckles to this idea. "You want to nickname *me*?" Despite the odd circumstances, Thevenin felt welcomed by Sympl. He nods, "Hah, alright! Call me *Volt* then."

The two companions exert a small laugh. After the joyful moment, they continue to look up at the dim sky. Yearning for a solution to leave the sinkhole's mighty abyss, Volt smirks, "Got any ideas on how to escape?"

. . .

Rallied up near the broken arena, the tense riot continues to glare at Zyra. "You're not going to take this, creep!" she sadly blurts back. She uses her free hand to gracefully hold onto her scarf. Some members took offense and drew their weapons directly at Zyra; they were hungry for action of some sort. Murmuring intensifies and Zyra takes a stance on herself.

"*Void Imporia*... I hate this place with every fiber of my bone. This damn election game and all the people in it can go to hell. If you want to be uncooperative, I will give you one more chance to reconsider our deal." the impatient masked man barges. Zyra refuses to comply while looking straight at the ground.

The masked man sees how vulnerable Zyra was. To this, he was quickly riddled with an uncomfortable sense upon glancing at Zyra's defeated look. A combination of her pose and expression reflects the image of someone he remembers dearly. Seeing this makes the masked man clear his throat. "I'll let the newest member of Aphotic do the honors." With this, the masked man summons the group's newest integrant. The crowd becomes silent. Members begin to look at each other in slight confusion. Vaguely, a man recklessly makes his way to the center of the crowd. "Yes sir, *Mister Blank*!" the voice excitingly bellows.

To Zyra's disbelief, she had locked her eyes on *Draw* — an ex-comrade gatekeeper. Once Draw reveals himself, he jokingly gasps, "Zyra? Looks like you got lucky during the hatchening!" Draw snickers. Draw's appearance was identical to Zyra's memory, with the exception of wearing a bright red scarf.

"This gentleman has been doing me a great favor. Telling me the secrets and capabilities of gatekeepers... How noble, isn't he?" Blank states, cracking a large grin. He places his drenched red hand over Draw's shoulder, "Both him and I agree that hit-markers are known for wearing red." Blank eerily calls. The grinning Draw chuckles, "Heh, you tell her, boss!" Without warning, Blank forcefully shoves Draw onto the ground.

The red gatekeeper hits the ground with a large thud. "What the—" Draw replies in uncertainty. The nervous Imporian begins to roll over only to freeze. Blank's bloody red arm transforms into a sharp javelin-like pin. Without hesitation, he forcefully stabs Draw's back, sticking him to the ground. The impaled Imporian screeches in pain.

"Don't move a damn muscle, otherwise it'll rip you apart." Blank coldly snarls. Draw reaches out his hand towards Zyra. He continues to scream in agony and barely articulates his words, "Z-Zyra! Help!" Shocked, Zyra simply gawks in repulsion.

"Aphotic, we shall rain death to anyone who gets in our way... Even if it is a noble gatekeeper of Imporia." Blank declares. The crowd then roars upon hearing the news. The tense-induced crowd finally loses their patience wildly swerves their weapons into the air. "So, are you really a traitor? I'd like to see you choose." Blank contently says.

The joyful leader and the roaring crowd only made Draw erratically sweat. "If you want to keep your precious scarf, I suggest ending this man's life." Blank commands. Zyra freezes upon hearing these words.

After finally laying her eyes on a familiar face, she is now forced to choose between a measly cloth that dangles on her neck or the life of a formal comrade. Yet, despite the speed and scale of the situation, Zyra recalls specific actions of the not-so-nice Draw. Times where the superior gatekeeper mocked her sword, ditched her in defenselessness and his constant bickering about her deplorable abilities rings in her head.

"Tick-tock, time it ticking. Save this traitor or please Aphotic?" he coldly adds. Mixed with emotions, Zyra feels the world spin around her. Her urges to get revenge on Draw were strongly evident, yet she refuses to honor the henchman's request.

The up-roaring riot chants, "Pull the scarf!" Draw continues to struggle on the cold floor. Blank reacts by thrusting his pin arm deeper into Draw's back. The Imporian screams louder only to be muted by the audience's chanting. "Well, what are you going to do?" Blank sinisterly questions.

An unsettling exhale comes out of Zyra. The guardian approaches the suffering Imporian. Draw's face is visibly in pain, yet he finds small relief seeing Zyra approach him. "P-Please...! I was only messing with y-you back then!" Draw painfully coughs. Without any emotion, Zyra bends towards his floored body.

"...You waste your breath on such mundane hope. Let me show you what being hopeless truly feels like." Zyra replies and agonizingly yanks his scarf out of his neck. With a grimace, she holds up the scarf for the crowd to see.

Without hesitating, Zyra confidently holds out the ex-gatekeeper's red scarf. Her pride rejuvenates her strong-willed attitude as she no longer grew anxious from the crowd. Her wicked self began to gather peace of mind as she finally found a way to humiliate her formal comrade. Granted his pained state, Zyra internally smiles to this.

A simple symbol of superiority secures Zyra's serenity.

Everyone surrounding her abruptly erupted. All members cheered and jeered at her actions. Zyra then whips out her sword and turns back at Draw. Before she could commit to another movement, he was screaming until his voice faded into nothing.

Draw had been evaporating directly in front of Zyra. Seeing this completely horrified her; how would she have known the consequences of unscarfing a survivor? It only took a few seconds for Draw's body to become colorful steam and disappear from the audience. Blank unsticks his pinned arm from the ground and reverts it back to its normal arm shape. He then applauds the frozen Zyra.

"Revenge is sweet, isn't it?" he rhetorically questions. Still in disbelief of what she had witnessed, Blank immediately demands another request. He instructs her to place the freshly yanked red cloth over her precious green one. Empty minded, she stays frozen until Blank repeats his demand. Out of terror, she does what is instructed of her to do.

First, she gradually places the red scarf on her neck then proceeds to wrap her guilt on her thin neck. "Good. Now untie your green scarf." Blank mutters. Didn't he pledge that she would be able to keep it? Had she been pressured into a corner? The command that Blank declares creates harsh resistance within Zyra's cold-blooded spirit. With absolute disbelief, Zyra blankly stares into nothingness, allowing her mind to wallow in what may result into a disastrous evaporation.

"I said, untie your green scarf, *Zyra*." Blank mutters again with an elevated aggression in his voice. Comprehending what may lay ahead, she gives up her will to be – how could she live with taint in her oath? Afterall, gatekeepers are saviors, not murders... She begins to untie the green scarf only to learn that she remains unaffected; Zyra did not vaporize into steam like her comrade did. "Beautiful." Blank smirks as he snatches the now loose green scarf.

Out of reaction, Zyra snaps out of her daze and attempts to snag back her innocent possession. However, by the time she reaches her hand out to the green scarf, Blank had already thrown it into the hungry crowd of blue-scarf-wearing Aphotic members.

In slow motion, Zyra sees the tainted-green scarf being devoured by the bumpy crowd. Members that wore a blue scarf trampled each other as they chased after the green yarn. Promptly, they begin to savagely war against one another in efforts to wear a more *valuable* color. Their hunger for a 'better' color puzzled Zyra. More importantly, the last tether she had of her despicable comrade now resides with her in the form of a red scarf.

Sluggishly realizing this in combination with the horrific evaporation she triggered causes her to puncture a tear. Before all of the cumulating stresses shatter through her shut eyes, Blank suddenly places his hand over her shoulder and releases a hearty chuckle. "Welcome to Aphotic." he says observing the faceless army wrestle each other for the green cloth.

The pale-struck traitor was breathing uncontrollably as she slowly curls herself down to her knees. With her eyes widen, hands over her head and guilt trickling over her face, Blank scorns her. "Get used to it, sweet-cheeks. It'll all be over before you know it." Still phased by seeing a recognizable associate evaporate into nothingness, Zyra begins to whisper to herself.

With a tad of empathy, Blank scoffs heavily. "Oh yeah, pretty important to let you know that from now on, you shall be called Zoraidia. It's for your own safety – Certain *threats* should not know your real name." – "Zoraidia..." Zyra unconsciously whispers in her broken state.

Zyra suddenly finds herself remembering images of burning flames. Draw's pained expression will forever be seared in Zyra's mind. Was Zyra's boiling anger against Draw taken to far? Will she ever find peace over this playful accident? Culpability daunts the now red-colored gatekeeper.

Chapter III:
Loose Voltage

What does freedom cost?

"You're telling me that you don't remember how you ended up in this ditch?" Volt interviews. "Affirmative." Sympl answers. Volt endlessly tackles Sympl with questions about his origins, abilities, and perspective of the world they inhabited. The more questions he asked, the more lost the trapped Imporian felt.

"None of this is adding up." Volt concludes. The trench's steep walls were simply unclimbable. The gaping surface continues to taunt the misplaced Imporian. Lastly, the unresponsive companion couldn't properly reason with Volt. The feeling of entrapment begins to bother Volt.

"...If it has been weeks, the bark would've attained a level of growth." Sympl comments on the state of the empty tree.

"...Did you really just take your fourth nap of the day? How? Are you okay?" Sympl questions after Volt yawns from a period of slumber.

"...The garden is whispering..." Sympl states, piquing Volt's interest. "Error, it was just an auditory hallucination." the robot proclaims.

"...Did you know that Sympl knows and feels sign language?" the robot randomly bursts, disturbing the longing silence. Volt playfully move his hands without thinking. "What do you mean you like to 'bite enclosed ink?'"

The compilation of commentaries that Sympl spoke continues to make Volt question his scenario. He ultimately stares at the blinding light above him. "Hey, Sympl... You think we're stuck here for a reason?" he questions at the aimless skies. "The consequence of our meeting is indeed relevant to the previous events of the current situation. Therefore, perhaps there may be a reason for all of this." the robot comments.

"No, like, do you think we're stranded because of something we *did*? Something *wrong*, maybe?" he continues to ask. Before the robot could input its thoughts, Volt sighs. "Actually, never mind. You don't even remember or know what Imporia is." He continues to gaze the white sky, "I just thought that, just maybe, this may be some really weird limbo of some sort..." he comments to himself.

Sympl doesn't respond to any of Volt's monologues; the robot just soaks in his words without contributing. The quiet Imporian then notices that near the surface, crumbs of dirt were falling apart. These bits of dirt crashed into the garden, alerting the duo.

Volt's eyes followed the trail of dirt. He opens his mouth in awe once he sees a small head poking out from the very top of the sinkhole. "Is anyone down there?" the voice from above quietly echoes. "W-What? Hey! I'm stuck!" Volt impulsively shouts, unable to hear the person's voice. The Imporian continues to yell at the top of his lungs in hopes to catch the stranger's attention. Upon hearing the Imporian's response, the stranger's lingering head disappears.

"H-Hey! Come back!" Volt bellows in desperation. Sympl then emits a gloomy beep, "Perhaps the person was intimidated by your looks." – "Looks? I couldn't see who that person was! How the heck would they see me?" Volt brashly replies. He then stomps in frustration, "You've got to be kidding me!" the furious Imporian yells.

"The first time someone real exists and—huh?"

Suddenly, something lightly tapped his hair. Jump-scared, Volt pounces up only to discover a long string of cloth dangling above him. The string had multiple colored cloths stitched to each other and led all the way to the surface. "Woah…" he comments under his breath. Sympl gives him the suggestion to use the rope to climb out of the sinkhole. Clearly, Volt didn't need anyone to tell him twice.

The Imporian latches his arms around the cloth and lightly yanks it. He notices that the stitches were extremely strong since they did not show any signs of weakness with his yanking. Momentarily, he places his foot on the rough walls of the sinkhole. As Volt places his other foot, he soon learns that Sympl's weight held him back.

He struggles to pull himself up. "Crap… Did I really gain that much weight?" he comments to himself. "Perhaps I may be able to provide assistance. To activate my extensive cables, tap my shell." The numerical voice spoke. Hesitant, Volt clumsily presses his palms onto Sympl's head. Immediately, the cables that straddled around his shoulders swooped under him. Sympl's wires had plugged themselves onto the wall, further supporting Volt's ability to climb. "Tactical Wires: Activated." Sympl announces.

With the cables behaving like an extra set of legs, Volt and Sympl begin to hike up the walls with ease. The Imporian was impressed with how his backpack companion could adapt its steamy wires to perform other tasks. Each step up the steep walls made Volt shine brighter as he neared the white skies. After a lot of struggling, Volt and Sympl had successfully escaped the sinkhole.

Reaching the surface, the escapist covers his eyes for a few moments. The shining colorless environment was contrary to the grim garden's dark shadows. To give Volt a moment to himself, Sympl retracts its stiff wires back into its shell. Free from tangled grips, Volt rubs his eyes and is then greeted by the person who threw the escape rope in the first place.

Meeting the stranger felt like a new experience; he shies at the saying anything immediately. Pondering the figure, he sees that this person had strange, bulky ears darting out of its feminine face. Her presence radiated warmth and welcoming, yet her appearance is one of a fabled creature of some sort – the Imporian had never seen such a figure. The lady he looked at had pale violet skin that was contrasting her dark dress and sleeves. A loud slipping sound was made at the entire string of cloth had retracted into the lady's sleeves. Not only did this make Volt squint his eyes at her sleeves, but he comprehends that she has an array of claws instead of normal, human fingers.

"Uh…" he stutters before Sympl lightly zaps him. "Y-You're a real lifesaver!" Volt exclaims after getting buzzed by his robotic backpack. Regardless of Sympl's gestures, his gratitude came off as genuine. The lady begins to sniff the escapist and gently slide her claws on his lavish scarf. Sympl spouts an alarm, "Error detected!" While this blurt startled Volt, the woman remains unfazed. "That color and that enrichening smell… Never seen fangs like these before…" she murmurs to herself. Tickled, Volt questions what the lady had been doing.

"Hey, that tickles…!" Volt nervously spouts. The lady stops her ticklish sniffing and gives him his personal space. The lady then giggles as she gradually pertains herself. In an uncomfortable delivery, Volt steps away from the clingy lady. He composes himself with a brief cough, "Sorry… So, uh, it's been a while and last time I checked, Imporia doesn't snow…" Volt adds once he observes that the island's surface was completely white and empty.

"Very silly observation, *Champion!* Welcome to the Void." the lady warmly smiles. "…Champion? Void?" he confusingly responds. Volt turns his neck back in an attempt to glance at Sympl who also nods in misunderstanding. "This unit is identified as '*Volt*,' not '*Champion*,' rescuer." Sympl beeps out. Hearing the voice of the robot speak in full sentences made the lady curious to see where the voice had come from. She lightly taps her claw onto Sympl's metallic structure only to be starstruck by the metallic clinging sound its hollow shell made.

"A robot in the void?" she interrogates. The robot flares another alarm, "Warning! An unidentified target has invaded personal space. Releasing Tactical—" the robot's monotone speech gets interrupted by Volt's stuttering. "C-Calm down, Sympl!" The lady smiles gently, "Sympl?" – "Yeah, don't mind Sympl. He's just as lost as I am." the escapist honestly replies. "Sympl, Sympl, Sympl… Does that ring a bell? Absolutely not!" she chants to herself.

He then stands still, letting the silence between the two of them grow. The noiseless lady doesn't do anything but silently stare at Volt.

"...Uh, so, what do you mean by the void?" Volt questions in an attempt to get answers.

Isn't it obvious? This empty land was the perfect target as the Hatchening's victim!

...The Hatchening?

Sounds like an egg...

Oh? Did you not see sky-cracks? Perhaps you were already slumbering too?

H-Hey! Were you the one responsible for that!?

Very adorable assumption, Champion!

However, I alone could not have performed such an event.

Well, by any chance, any idea who or what caused it?

What would you do to the offender, Champion?

Her question rings in his head. What would he do? More importantly, what *could* he do? Volt hustles himself and thinks for a moment. "What would I do? Well, for starters, I'd tell them to put everything back to normal!" Volt mindlessly states as the lady giggles quietly. "What's so funny?" Volt asks.

"I just haven't felt this alive before! Besides, go back to normal? Why would anyone want to go back to sleeping forever again?" the lady spouts. Volt scratches his head to her odd responses. She continues to warmly smile at the Imporian without blinking. "I'm mean, I'm excited to finally get to see someone after all this time too! But your staring is uh..." Volt shrugs as Sympl beeps "Volt is not feeling the same frequency with you unlike me." the robot bluntly says. She responsively giggles then turns around to stop staring.

"Sympl! That's not what I mean to say..." Volt sluggishly adds.

"Okay, nevermind. I'm just really out of touch, so sorry about the whole gap. Anyway, what about me being a champion? Is there like a competition going on or something?" Volt questions. The patient lady hides her arms and takes small skips, "Correct! The winner gets *another chance at happiness,* and so far, you're winning!"

"Wait, I'm winning another chance at happiness? What do you mean? How the heck am I winning anything?" the puzzled Imporian continues to ask without hesitating. "You're going to be blessed with a wonderful opportunity if you continue to hold your title as champion." she mysteriously states once again. "Look, that's not helping me understand anything." Volt bluntly says.

Once again, the lady remains patient and quiet as she could not contain her large smile. "We're both beautiful strangers! If you keep asking questions, it'll be harder for us to move on." she playfully replies. The dumbfounded Volt squints at her confusingly, "Okay seriously, what is your deal?" — "Well, if you're tired of me talking about the *election*, then I'll jump straight to introductions!" the lady says as she wistfully turns around.

"You may call me *Ophelia*, my dear champion."

"I'm looking for the champion who wears the fabled *velvet scarf*." the bubbly rescuer confidently states. "It's a matter of life or no life if you do not wish to cooperate with my needs." she adds.

"Election? Velvet scarf? Now I'm more lost than before!" Volt claims once he crosses his arms. Ophelia giggles again. She playfully twirls around the perplexed escapist. "In Void Imporia, a scarfer who wears a velvet scarf is to be elected as a champion, thus winning another chance at happiness." she clarifies. "In other words, a very special event will happen to you soon since you are considered a champion, Champion!"

Bewildered by her words, Volt smirks lightly. "See, even though none of that makes sense, I'm starting to understand what you're trying to say." he comments. "Are you telling me that I'm winning something that'll make me, uh, happy? Or are you just really bad at flirting?" Volt asks for clarification as Ophelia silently winces.

"Volt, if this is getting too convoluted, I have been documenting all speech sequences. Currently, they are logged into my personal diary, that only you are able to see. If you wish to replay an answer to a question, simply request it and I shall replay the appropriate soundbites." Sympl budges. "...How long have you been recording?" the Imporian pops the question with the robot replying with, "Since the reboot." Volt inaudibly gasps and embarrassingly stammers, "E-Everything?" Ophelia laughs hearing this as she lightheartedly slaps Volt on the chest. "You're very silly, you know?" she confesses.

"...Anyway, what do you mean by a velvet scarf?" Volt uncomfortably shrugs. He then glances at his loose flaps to see the magenta color he had been wearing. "That sounds like what I'm wearing... I mean, it was grey before it became this color. Like I took a bite from—" Volt explains right as Ophelia interrupts him. "Silly, its normal for all scarfs start out as grey. Once the election begins, scarf-wearers are randomly assigned to their colors." Ophelia sneers. "Looks like you're the lucky one here." she adds seductively.

"Sure…" Volt uncertainly replies. Volt's hassle at asking more questions with unsatisfying answers makes him pause the conversation. He then unlocks his sight at Ophelia and begins to stare into aimless directions of the void. He continues to see nothing with the exception of some water-colored patches floating at the far distance. He attempts to ask Ophelia what those patches were, getting yet another odd response. "The void isn't cleaned up just yet." she says in slight agitation.

Volt begins to stretch his arms. "Well, this really is a weird—*WOAH*! What in the name of Imporia is that!?" The Imporian shoots his head up and witnesses the large star-shaped ribbon floating in the sky. "Astra…" Ophelia calmly replies. "How the heck didn't I notice it sooner? It's so beautiful!" he shouts in excitement. Despite the commentary, Ophelia replies again. "Am I really *that* alluring?" she flirtatiously asks.

Uncomfortable at her suggestions, Volt weakly chuckles. "So, if you know what it is, then like, what does it do?" he finds himself asking more questions knowing that he wouldn't get a proper answer. Out of curiosity, the Imporian still tries to learn about his environment. "That's a surprise for you to learn later." Ophelia joyfully responds with a wink.

"Are you hiding something from me...?" Volt questions. The Imporian has a hard time understanding Ophelia's intentions. Her heroism finally enables his freedom, yet the onboarding of the Astra's presence overwhelmed his reality. "Nothing will be hidden from you – the reason is all in plain sight." Ophelia replies.

"Don't get the wrong idea, Champion! I may be an open book, but if I told you all of my secrets, then I would be very embarrassed!" Ophelia sheepishly adds. With his arms on his hips, Volt leans in and continues his endless questioning. "I don't know... You definitely know something's up." – "The Astra, no?" Ophelia replies.

Gullible Volt gets done-goofed. "Okay, fine. Just answer me this! Election, velvet scarf, another pants at happiness, Astra – that's a lot to take in. But how come my hunger is constant even after I ate those—" Volt gets interrupted as Ophelia blurts, "Silly! You should know that the void deprives you of urges too! I can't remember when was the last time I had visited a restroom!" Ophelia interrupts once again.

"Too much information." Sympl sassily spouts. "No urges either? What is this, the after-life?" Volt goofily questions. "Bingo!" Ophelia cheerfully replies.

Volt releases a light chuckle that gradually silences itself into apprehension. He then carefully takes her statement and analyzes the entire environment he's been first-handedly experiencing. His forehead sweats a bit in the realization that Ophelia may be the most transparent person he's ever interacted with. Finally, he begins to shake.

"...You're kidding right?" Volt questions.

"Champion, do you doubt my words?" Ophelia eerily questions. Volt trembles upon hearing her heed. "Unstable movement detected." Sympl alerts, making Ophelia's cold expression one into curiosity. She gets closer to the stiffened body in efforts to inspect his robotic companion. "...How about you, 'Sympl?' Can you detect an error in my honesty?" she genuinely asks as the robot remains silent. "Mmm... You have a really good grasp of Champion's back, huh?" She comments.

The now-freed-but-disturbed escapist begins to take footsteps at erratic directions. His nervousness and indecisive footing slowly push him away from the prophet who unearth too much harmful knowledge. "Ophelia... I think I'm going to be sick." Volt queasily says as he sees himself drifting away from her presence.

"You can't get sick either, silly!" Ophelia snorts. "In fact, when you think about it, this is the perfect place to settle down on! No urges imply a lot of beautiful aspects, Champion!" Noticing that Volt was leaving the scene, she lightly jogs to his leaving position. "Where are you going, Champion?"

Volt hesitates to answer. Between the trickling sweat and how he felt that his gravity was off-center, the dizzy Imporian desperately desires to get some fresh air. "Are you feeling that bad? We can talk it out!" Ophelia cheerfully responds before Volt slipped out of her grasp.

"This can't be! This can't be the same Imporia I've always known!" the panicky Imporian lies to himself. "Wait, what about the islanders? Where are they?" Volt frantically spouts. Ophelia empathizes with the flustered champion as she attempts to comfort him with a gentle glint. "Islanders? There is no such thing as islanders, champion. At least, I haven't encountered any survivors besides yourself. That being said—"

"Survivors!? N-No! This is a mistake! The islanders are still here, right? They have to be in the plaza! And the watchtower! The gatekeepers are still there! They have to be intact, right!?" Volt hysterically erupts. His heart races upon pondering what had happened to the jolly islanders. "Why are you so worried about something that doesn't exist anymore?" Ophelia questions out of inquisitiveness.

Without a proper response to her prompts, Volt simply runs off into the distance. Ultimately leaving Ophelia behind in exchange to see what the island had become, Volt dismisses his rescuer without any regards. This draws a frown on Ophelia's face. She ensures that the coast is clear before speaking to herself.

Being ignored again, huh? Disobedience requires punishment.

Must we change tactics this early on already? Champion appears to be very kind and compassionate…

43

Chapter IV:
Aphotic – a Legion of Misery

Who are your teammates in this life?

Well, how's the armor? Can you move freely?

Yeah, yeah. Lighter than expected.

Hah, well, welcome to the Ayamox Fort!

Woah! Isn't this where the gatekeepers live?

Used to, lad. But we're safe here because –

Cut the sweet talk, pops. Where's my weapon?

Oh? Reza, why don't you take a moment to learn about the Ayamox –

You promised me a weapon to defend Amphy and myself.

Well yes, but you need—

"Remember that we're here to work together!" Hand it over already, ya' coop.

Grant senses her spiteful attitude as if she were still uncomfortable with the idea of helping strangers. While the two were discussing their deals, Amphy playfully cartwheels around the garden. The child couldn't help but enjoy what little nature was left in Void Imporia.

"Amphy! Behave yourself." Reza intensely mumbles. The young child was too immersed with his ragdoll to listen to his sister's low voice. Grant intervenes with, "The boy probably has a lot on his mind right now. Why don't you let him relax a little?" Upon arguing, Grant gently places his hand on her head. To this, Reza immediately dishes out his wrinkled hands. "Don't touch me!" she erupts.

Disheartened at her lash out, Grant takes a deep breath, "I apologize, Reza." He stands in silence, allowing Reza to briefly reflect her barking attitude. She quickly grows guilty but hides her remorse. "...Weapon?" she words, trying to channel away her culpability.

"I know you want a tool to defend yourself and your child, but—" The elder empathizes only to get cut off. "Child!? Amphy is my *little brother!* How dare you assume I'd do something that vulgar for my age!" Reza erupts yet again. Grant puts his hands in front of himself, trying to calm her down. "Listen, I believe you have some issues you need to sort out." the elder sheepishly confesses.

"Issues!?" Reza shouts. Members of the Ayamox fort were busy handling their assigned tasks until they overheard Reza's lurid yelling. Soaking in the heat of the argument, Grant grows a bit red. "Reza, please, comport yourself. How can I trust you with a weapon if you can't handle a one to one conversation?" Grant questions. "Well maybe if you minded your own business I wouldn't be biting." she replies, crossing her arms.

Please calm down. How can I arm you when you're ang—

Are you really bringing up anger issues as an excuse to not arm me?

Well no, but you need—

Then stop with the excuses and hand me a damn weapon already.

I'll fetch you the best thing we have.

Those hunters will ever know what'll hit 'em!

Grant releases a blaring whistle and curls his index finger, signaling his comrades to bring her what she heavily desired. Eventually, two armored figures decorated with a similar uniform as Reza walk towards the duo. Of the figures, one carried a towering, unidentifiable object.

Once they reached close quarters, the figures revealed a husky man and an older woman. Reza then realizes it was the same couple who previously cleared the coast in the hunter's last ambush.

Reza observes the metallic staff only to realize it had an odd stroke of hair coming out from the top. "...Who the hell fights with a paintbrush?" she questions, almost sarcastically. "No really, you expect me to tickle people to death?" Her eruptive commentary makes the group go awkwardly quiet. "Reza, this is what was left. This fort had a lot of left-over armor and tools, but one can only assume that most weapons were taken. Does this not suffice?" Grant annoyingly questions with his gritting teeth. "It's an oversized paintbrush." she states blankly. "Yes, but you can use it to fend for yourself." Grant replies with much more ease.

"Oh, I get it. You don't *trust* me with a sword?" she mocking bullies the elder again. "Reza, we don't have swords. What you see is what you get. Be grateful for it." Grant slowly begins to lose his patience as he gripped his cane even harder. "You're expecting me to go back out there with a paintbrush? Dude, is this a joke? Do you want me to paint this empty canvas with this? Is that your plan?" Reza continues to dart her rude commentaries towards the agitated elder.

In the distance, Amphy bashfully toys around inside the crumbling fort with his doll. The imaginative boy uses his doll as a sort of action figure, hopping around his surroundings with a focus on his beloved figurine. His role-playing eventually bumps him into strangers who were in the middle of a diplomatic conversation. The boy grows shy again, but once the unfamiliar strangers compliment the boy's ragdoll, he easily opens up to their words. Amphy eavesdrops to hear the members discussing their current project.

After hearing the compassionate stranger's plans, the giddy boy jogs back to the outer area of the fort. Once he sees Reza, Grant, and two other figures, the jolly child runs up to her. "Reza!" Amphy springs up, "These people are trying to make a rainbow with the scarves!" the young boy energetically announces. Grant feels Amphy's contagious enthusiasm and cracks a large smile. "Ah yes, our rainbow theory..." the elder speaks. The husky man directly looks at Reza and hands over a large paintbrush-like staff he had been holding.

Rainbow theory? Tools to paint? Reza's mind boggles in questions and concerns that she could not comprehend. "*Allena*, *Hassen*, why don't you explain the rainbow theory to the siblings?" the elder suggests. His opportunity in introducing the two guardians indirectly cools him off from Reza's impolite bashing.

"Of course!" Allena cheerfully states. "We've noticed that everyone we've faced had one thing in common, which is, a scarf. Grant has theorized that these scarfs may be the answer to escaping this void." Allena explains. Amphy jumps up, "Oh! But why a rainbow?" poking a curious question into the conversation. Hassen releases a hardy chuckle and crotches down to the young boy. "Whenever you see a rainbow, you cast a wish, right?"

The bulky guardian continues to explain while pointing his index finger at the floating Astra, "Well, those ribbons closely resemble a rainbow. We've all figured out that if we were to make a scarf holding all colors, perhaps we could get our wish of escaping to come true or even find a solution with this." he announces.

Reza hysterically cackles to herself before erupting. "...Pfft! That's the dumbest sentence I've ever heard in my life!" Reza carelessly complains followed by an outburst of laughter. "Really? Do you think some random-ass combination of colors is going to magically get us out of this hell-hole? Do you think that some artificial wishing can get us out? You're all really hopeless." she heartlessly lashes out. Everyone remains silent, except Grant who raises his voice.

"Dammit, Reza! I'm willing to do this to see my family again, okay!?" the old man spouts, creating a worse silence. He then takes a deep breath, hushing the impulsive commentator. Induced by fear, Amphy hides behind Reza's dress. Everyone around the Ayamox base who witnesses Grant's yelling stood in shock. Some unidentified members even sudden mourn about the thought of their loved ones.

This wasn't an easy process for anyone to deal with. No one was freed of the trauma the hatchening had induced. Isolation, mystery, and impending doom wafts around the open airs of Void Imporia. Yet, what merit did these hopeless Imporian have? Could such an idea ever work?

Reza froze seeing the affectionate, patient elder snap. "We don't have answers, we don't have clues and we don't even have time. Please, this is one thing that all of us agree on." He says with his hand trembling on his cane. "Even if we really are desperate, we've all been separated from something precious to us, and I'm trying to get it back." Grant shakenly says.

Reza musters up the audacity to slowly apologize for her wedging attitude. Grant takes a moment to calm himself. "...No, I should be apologizing. I'm sorry for forcing you to join us. I just figured that, y'know, you'd want to go back home too." the elder confesses.

Full of guilt, Reza avoids eye contact with the angry elder. With a sigh, the elder asks, "Do you have any other better ideas?" Reza nods negatively. "N-No... Maybe you're right. Sorry..." she sheepishly replies. "Very well... Allow me to assign you your grand task. The faster we get it done, the more time we have to experiment." Grant reinforces as he clears his throat.

"Hold your horses! I'm not going alone out there." Reza spouts. "Worry not, Reza. Allena and Hassen will accompany you to our safest location." Grant adds. Could she afford to entrust her safety with two complete strangers? Regardless of their redeeming track-record, Amphy's precious eyes reassure Reza's priorities. She must keep her promise, *right?*

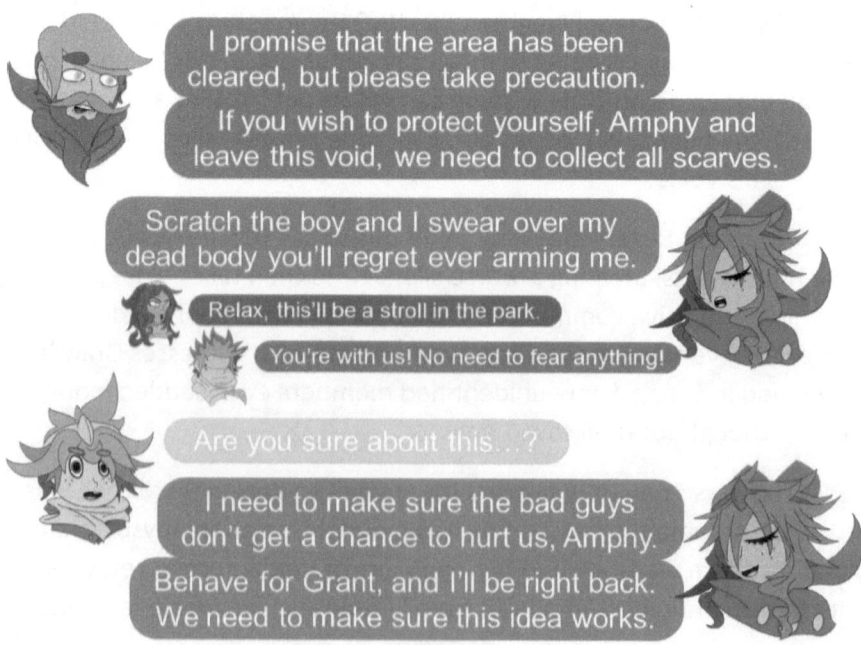

I promise that the area has been cleared, but please take precaution.

If you wish to protect yourself, Amphy and leave this void, we need to collect all scarves.

Scratch the boy and I swear over my dead body you'll regret ever arming me.

Relax, this'll be a stroll in the park.

You're with us! No need to fear anything!

Are you sure about this...?

I need to make sure the bad guys don't get a chance to hurt us, Amphy.

Behave for Grant, and I'll be right back. We need to make sure this idea works.

Meanwhile, Aphotic had been patiently waiting for their leader's commands. Like an orchestrator, Blank conducts and sorts out his entire legion with a few hand signals. Groups were formulated by the color of their scarves and were eventually dismissed to follow the duties the leader had assigned.

"We are to reunite at the arena every time one of the appendages roll up!" Blank confidently announces. Completely unaware of what anything meant, Zyra gloomily sits in the arena's bleachers only to soak in her deep thoughts. She distances herself from everyone in the arena, reflecting on what she has done so far.

Her hunched position and zoned-out expression prevented her from seeing an Aphotic member who sits right next to her. This figure then scoots in, yet fails to catch Zyra's attention. A constant inhaling muffles near Zyra, eventually snapping her out of her aimless gaze.

What type of mask was Zyra staring at?

"Why the dreadful face?" the feminine voice greets. The lady wore a mask that mimicked Blank's faceplate. However, her blank mask was covered in slabs of ink, specifically to resemble eyes and a mouth. She had thick hair in the form of a donut. Ponytails rolled out of it and were held by a red and green object that resembled a jewel. Her unusual flimsy body and yarn-like hair gave her literal doll vibes. One of her most unique features was the fact that she wore two scarfs – a red and green cloth. Observing the puppet-looking lady awakens Zyra from her gloomy thoughts.

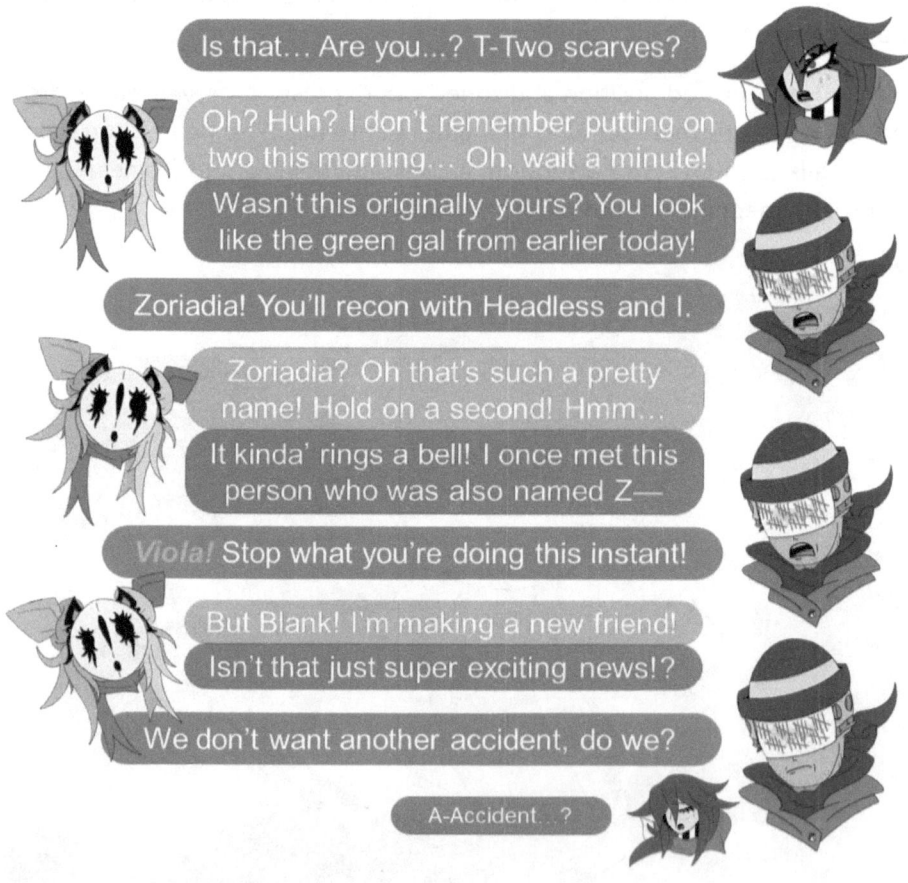

Zyra snaps out of her shocked state and calmly makes her way down towards the center of the arena. She reunites herself with Blank and finds herself next to one more member who wore a highlighting yellow scarf. Blank then nears Zyra to whisper a few words. "Whatever you do, do not talk to that puppet. Once she starts, she'll never shut her trap." Extremely confused, Zyra glances back to see Viola waving back at them.

"What do you mean by accident then…?" – "Just don't get near her if you want to keep your scarf." Blank barks back.

"Blank, I have a lot of questions…" Zyra softly raises her voice.

"Whatever it is, make it quick. We're running out of time." the leader hassles. "Can you please tell me why did Draw evaporate when I took off his scarf?" Hearing this makes Blank scoff, "Drawicus? You made a statement about traitors, no? You are to never mention the name of a traitor, you got that?" – "I want answers." Zyra demands.

Blank snickers and begins to compliments her demanding attitude, "Heh, you really are as serious as those pesky gatekeepers." Unphased by that phrase, Zyra pouts. "Why did *he* evaporate?" she repeats mildly annoyed. "He's a weakling. It's better not to waste energy on freeloaders." the masked man declares. "*Weakling*…?" Zyra whispers to herself.

"Weakling!? Draw may be a prick, but he isn't weak! You can't just take off a piece of clothing and then lose the composition of your own body! How does that even make sense to you?" Zyra aggressively cries out as the frustration in her face grows more visible. "Do you want to stop people from melting?" Blank retaliates as Zyra grows silent.

"Drawicus can burn in hell. The poor chap claims he's a strong gatekeeper, but I've never seen someone betray their own comrade. He didn't even hesitate and desperately showed off how willing he was ready to tear *you* apart. It's why he has no place in Aphotic or this damn void – he's too… What's the word? *Competitive*." Blank grits.

"Yeah? Then what about those that were beating each other up for my scarf? Explain that!" Zyra exclaims with Blank cracking a smirk. "Exactly my point – traitors have no place in this world. Those who wear blue can also rot to ashes. In fact, don't ever expect anything from someone who wears blue. Blue barely has any value in this void anyway…"

Hearing this insane statement from the leader who guises himself with a mask continues to disturb Zyra. She glances at her blade and then scans the arena, but easily concludes that she logically cannot act impulsively. She was outnumbered to begin with and that doesn't seem to change any time soon either.

The leader then adjusts his vest and directly looks at the other member, *Headless*. "Are we done with the chit-chat? People die all the time – it shouldn't distract you. If you want to stop these damn scarves form melting everyone upon release, then I suggest you listening up." Blank remarks seriously. Zyra's attention had been clearly aligned with his peculiar wording. She simply couldn't shake off his attitude towards those that associated with him – does he truly care about his legion?

"Zoriadia, Headless, or as I should say, *hit markers*. As you should be aware, Aphotic is out searching for a specific magenta strap of cloth. We are to spread thin and increase our probabilities of tangible results. The sooner we detain our golden ticket, the better the results." Blank sloppily announces.

"Understood, Mister Blank." Headless responds quickly. "And what are you precisely expecting of me?" Zyra questions shamelessly. "The sword you wield."

Some unknown time later, Reza ventures with Hassen and Allena through the empty void. In the search of colorful cloth, Reza complains about her oversized paintbrush. "You guys *had* to take all the cool weapons and leave me with this thing." Reza sassily states. "Maybe if you didn't take forever to choose sides you wouldn't get leftovers." Hassen harshly replies. The trio ends up exploring an abandoned water-colored town.

"Plazas are normally full of people, so we should be able to find something laying around, right?" Allena hopefully alludes. In their quiet walking, Reza could hear a faint chatter from the distance. Impulsively, she crouches on her knees, "Yo! We're not alone…" she nervously announces. The armored lady then barely crawls to a broken wall. Allen and Hassen follow her footsteps since they too were intimidated by looming threats.

In the wall that Reza took cover at, she slowly pokes her head up to search for the voice. Allena and Hassen lay their backs on the barrier, letting Reza perform her recon. Skeptical for whatever had been chattering, the trio prepares for an ambush. Once Reza pokes her face out of the assembly of bricks, she catches a glimpse of a person wearing an extraordinarily large scarf, staring blankly at the devoided plaza.

The group eavesdrop at the duo's conversation.

Volt scans the area in depression. What was once a plaza full of festivity resides in ruins. Broken structures, hollow streets, and decimated plants haunt the phased Imporian. "Volt, this place is so much roomier than the sinkhole we were in, don't you think?" Sympl joyfully asks as Volt silently soaks in the empty void.

"Sympl... This plaza..." the Imporian anxiously states. Gazing his lost homeland, he quickly shakes himself in denial. "...N-No! That Ophelia chick is out of her mind! This can't be Imporia, impossible!" Volt comments with his arms crossed. "This is all just some weird prank, right?" Volt sheepishly asks with doubt in his voice.

"Prank?" – "Yeah... Like a big joke!" Volt shoots back. "Oh, like when you were kidnapped?" Sympl questions. "...Huh? Kidnapped? Me?" Volt confusingly questions in awe. "It's okay because you're awake now." Sympl replies. Volt stood frozen at the robot's ability to comprehend the term 'prank.' However, an undetected snort bursts from the duo's distance.

"Har-har, Sympl... You got the idea, but *afterlife*? Like are you for real? Ophelia can't actually tell us that with a straight face!" he speaks with skepticism. The Imporian continues to ignorantly deny the reality he's immersed himself with. The burdensome backpack beeps, ready to respond. "Apparently, Ophelia's data-log record suggests that the scarf may be a critical issue. Taking it off would result in the loss of the champion status." – "Are you telling me I should take it off and move on already? Would that reveal the prank?" the Imporian responds as he grabs a loose flap.

"Are you hearing this? This man wants to take his own life!" Reza brashly whispers. Allena then clenches her staff tightly, "Shh! Let him do it!" she argues. Reza gives her comrade a baffled look, "W-What? No! That's wrong!" In disbelief from Allena's cruel commentary, she frowns at the arguing duo. "Listen, we've never seen a magenta-colored scarf before. If he decides to forfeit his own life, then technically we don't have to get our hands dirty." Hassen adds.

"That's not fair though! He most likely doesn't even know the consequences of dropping that scarf!" Reza speaks in a horrified tone, breaking the whispering silence. "Too bad! That's his problem! We're here to collect leftovers so let's wait for him to do something stupid." Allena grudges. The tone of the trio began to grow more hostile as Allena and

Hassen viciously glare at Reza. "What happened to saving survivors!?" Reza blurts.

Volt continues to gaze at his flap only to be alerted by Sympl's beeping. "Error detected!" the robotic voice screeches, making Volt jump in the process. "Huh? What happened this time?" the scared Imporian asks. He frantically moves his head around the area in search of an answer to Sympl's alert. "Volt, I am detecting a vibrating disturbance nearby." Sympl declares. The frantic Imporian remembers the ground trembling below him, "What? Another earthquake?" Volt sheepishly questions.

"Negative. The vibrations are more relative to voices." Sympl concludes. This makes Volt less frantic but doesn't calm him down. "Voices? Someone is here!? Who's there?" Volt spouts and searches for nearby hiding locations. "Just... Just show yourself!" he adds with more tranquility. The velvet scarfer gets jumpy about the thought of finding someone hiding from him. Reza angrily whispers to her comrades, "He's going to keep his scarf and that's that!" Allena holds her down to prevent her from obliging to Volt's commands. Resisting Allena's tugging, Reza stood up and reveals herself to Volt in a matter of seconds.

Detecting an approaching person, Sympl automatically releases its tactical cables. The robotic wires gracefully wrap under each loose flap and weaponized Volt's scarf. The intimidating pose worries Reza, however, she softly responds with, "H-Hey, relax! I just want to talk."

Braced for anything, Volt scans Reza extremely carefully. His heart begins to race from the adrenaline of encountering another person in the void. Yet, he progressively grew more concerned upon analyzing her appearance. Her shoulder pads, although a different color from his, were identical to his. Her enormous paint-brush-like weapon reminded him of one of his comrade's weapons. As well, her navy-blue skin-protector also was matching Volt's skin protector. A sense of nostalgia hits Volt when observing Reza's familiar outfit. However, he couldn't help conclude that something *had* to happen to the previous owner of the outfit.

Is the lady wearing the armor of a gatekeeper an imposter? Did she do something wrong to previous owner? Is her appearance a warning for what's to come? Questions flood Volt's mind. Realizing the potential threat Reza may be, the two commence a decisive stare-off.

I've been warned about you!

Warned!? What do you mean?

My scarf, you want it. I know it!

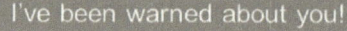
Shoot, he heard us!
Not he hasn't, shush!

What!? I'm here to tell you that you *shouldn't* take off your scarf!

I didn't plan to anyway. So what's the big idea?

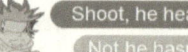
Was I this stubborn with Grant?
Sympl, scan her or something!

I'm trying to help you! You should really be a bit more grateful before bashing me up!

Volt, perhaps she is indeed speaking the truth.

Mmm… Nah, she definitely wants it.

If you must know, I'm just collecting unused cloth — I'm not going to take yours.

And why the heck are you collecting cloth? Are you a part of the election?

Election? The heck are we voting for? Sack of potatoes?

56

The skeptic Imporian stands up straight, breaking away from his hunched position. Seeing her adrift eyes and pacified persistency softens his tensed mood. "Garsh! Looks like I'm not the only lost one." Volt spews in tranquility. "Tell me about it..." Reza gently replies with less pressure.

"I'm sorry if I scared you! It's not the usual me! I've just been a bit confused on a couple of things and I'm just glad you're here and safe..." Volt begins to speak with a more relaxed tone. "I-It's all good, magenta dude. Truth be told, I've never seen a, uh, well, what exactly are you?" Reza brashly asks. Volt chuckles. "Oh, my bad! I never wear all of my armor, so that's probably why you're confused. I'm a gatekeep—"

The robotic backpack emits two minor buzzes, tickling Volt in the process. Suddenly, it flares an alert, "Warning!" Before Sympl could finish bursting its report, Hassen and Allena spiral into the air. Airborne for a brief moment, the duo strikes their staffs at Volt's direction. Sympl's cable arms swing in the exact opposite direction of the intended attack. Frightened, the Imporian loses balance. As he nearly trips, the remaining flaps that Sympl controls caught his balance.

A barrage of clashes went off.

Volt bounces back onto his feet. Allena and Hassan continue to push their staffs against Sympl's guarding cables. The Imporian then thrusts himself at the ambushers, pushing them off of his personal space. Evidently, his vigorous push forces them to back off. He then snaps his head at Reza's direction. "You liar!" he distressfully roars. In haste, Volt sprints away from the trio. Sympl uses its wires like legs, allowing Volt to boost his speed.

In absolute disbelief, Reza stares at the escaping Imporian. She then gawks and glares at her nasty comrades, "Hey! What the hell was that for!?" Reza explodes. Hassen points a finger at her and barks, "What do you mean, 'what the hell?' You let the magenta color get away!"

Chapter V:
Discreet Betrayal Rule

Loyalty or Death?

In the depths of Void Imporia, Zyra finds herself marching in the colorless island. Each footstep the gatekeeper takes deepens with regret. The haunting of her fallen comrade continues to silently bug her. What are Aphotic's real intentions? She continues to silently wonder to herself.

She was too intimidated to challenge the leader's authority, yet craves to learn her role. In a world where she could not lose anything, Zyra clears her throat. "Blank, we need to talk..." Zyra timidly speaks up. The masked man halts his movements and churns at the gatekeeper. Before he could respond, he holds out his hand, indicating for the crew to stop their movements. The masked man notices a stranger in a close radius.

The masked man gets flustered. His blood begins to boil, thus transforming his red-sleeved hands into one arm-sized pin. Witnessing the conversion makes Zyra take a step back out of repugnance.

"You're not supposed to be here...!" Blank harshly mutters. "Oh? Are you sure about that? What about you? Weren't you also supposed to stay where you came from?" Ophelia replies with jerkiness in her voice. Blank continues to approach the sarcastic target. "...No matter, it won't make a difference if you're here or not anyway..." Blank cackles as he converts his arm's flesh-wounds into sharp spikes.

"Because now, I finally get to maul you down like the pig you are." Blank happily states. Ophelia giggles and tilts her head. "Oink, oink! You think I'm a pig? Well, didn't your partner in crime abandon you for—" Ophelia gets interrupted by the masked man's blurt. "Shut the hell up!" To this, the entire crowd confusingly wonders upon the prophet's statement.

Unlike your cruel methods, I've actually gathered a team to end *your* election.

Wow! You dedicated a whole fanbase to me!? Isn't that so sweet of you?

...What is up with her?

Unfortunately for you, you can't stop me because we're on the same team, silly!

The hell are you talking about?

I wear red, you wear red, she wears red. We all wear *red!* Rad, right?

Expect for your faceless friend there...

Your point?

Unscarf me and you'll perish *with* me! That's what teammates are for, right?

You're bluffing.

Ophelia continues to taunt the masked man. "You're just mad that you can't release all of that pent-up anger on me, huh? I can see it on your face!" Immediately, Blank cockily points his pins at the snickering imp. "I can see these hands tearing you into bloody pieces." he snarls. The rouge imp then taps her red claws onto his deformed arms. "Nah-uh-uh! I just said that friendly fire will eliminate you from the election! Both of us are wearing red, silly!" Ophelia giggles.

"I'm flattered you want to get your hands dirty for me! But it's best not to get down and dirty this soon!" the frisky prophet winks, lowering his stance. "Headless? Mind doing the honors?" the leader blatantly requests his yellow-scarfed henchman to directly attack Ophelia. "Mm? You really came prepared this time, huh?" Ophelia giggles.

"As you wish, Mister Blank." Headless replies. "Is that why you all wear masks? You like being blind to your sins?" Ophelia playfully fumble. "Or is it because you don't want them to see their tragic fate?" Ophelia squeals in excitement. Blank recoils upon hearing her piercing words.

"Blanky-poo, if you get rid of me, *your most valuable ally*, then how will you ever know where to find the velvet scarf?" Ophelia titters. Blank carefully scans her crown and shutters. "Do not want to know *every* secret there is, Blanky-poo?" she deviously repeats. The crown shines upon Blank's mask as he remains silent. "Ridding me would be *regretful*..." she adds.

Headless and Zyra observe how the silent leader begins to subtly tremble. To this, Zyra slowly churns towards Headless, "What is his problem?" she whispers. Headless confidently replies with "That person is the sole reason why Aphotic exists. I must eliminate her." Concerned with the faceless men in the scene, Zyra tightly holds onto her blade.

"...Or are you forgetting everything again?" Ophelia continues to comment, agitating the shocked leader. "H-Hold on, Headless..." Blank mutters. With his lack of patience, Blank silently glares at the light-hearted Ophelia. "Mm! So, you do want to know more, yes?" the giddy Ophelia asks. "You know who is going to win the election, don't you?" Blank darts.

Teehee! I'm flattered you think I'm capable of doing ambitious stuff!

No one — *especially you* — should win another chance at happiness.

...Another chance at happiness?

"At the end of time, the one who wears the champion's scarf shall win the election and thus be granted another chance at happiness."

And does that *actually* mean?

It means that Ophelia is a horrendous person who needs to be dispatched this instant!

Blanky-poo, the champion wears *magenta*. Do you see me wearing pink?

I can see you wearing red in a second!

"Enough already!" Zyra spouts. The heavy weight of losing a comrade makes her hunch over in guilt. With too many warnings and violence, Zyra tries to break away any sudden attacks. "If you think she's behind some scheme or something, you yourself have a lot to clarify, mister." Zyra directs at Blank. The masked leader grunts as he simply turns away. Blank's veins start to show up on his neck as his blood boils.

"Zoraidia, shut up." Blank mutters as Zyra scoffs, "You're acting like a child! You don't have a reason to slash someone who hasn't directly done anything to you!" Zyra baffles. Instantly, Blank darts his pin-arm near Zyra's foot causing her to flinch. Alarming Headless, Blank faces the ground pathetically. "You know nothing about that witch."

"Witch...?" Zyra questions silently. "No sweetheart, I'm a pig, remember?" Ophelia jokingly adds as she directly stares at Zyra. Letting this mysterious figure glare at Zyra with such confidence causes Zyra to get a bit nervous. The shaky gatekeeper remains silent as Ophelia continues to scan Zyra's red scarf from a distance. "Very interesting..." Ophelia mutters to herself as she relocks her winking eye at Blank.

"Welp! I do have good news to tell you!" Ophelia smiles, unphased from Blank's brutal movements. "Good news doesn't exist anymore." Blank rages as he aims his direction towards the giggling prophet. "Put your chin up, Blanky-poo! Instead of using me as your dream punching bag, why don't you aim your target at the monster who has the velvet scarf?" Ophelia tattles.

Blank releases his locked pins near Zyra, giving the gatekeeper room to breathe. She trickles in sweat as her anxiety flew off the charts, yet maintained composure. She quietly pants to herself as her reasons to defend Blank diminished. How could this impulsive, blood-boiling-masking-wearing-self-proclaimed 'leader' dare strike at the one he requested for help? Zyra struggles to keep calm as Ophelia continues her speech.

Zyra's piquing anxiety continues to soar as she uncovers the fable of a 'wild-fanged monster' roaming the same void as her. Could her day not get any worse? "Ah, but don't worry too much about it! I'm confident you and your fanbase can take him down!" Ophelia snickers.

Instantly, her crown appears to slide off a bit out of its stiff position. She then gently places her claws over her head, fixing the offset of the crown. "Oh... In fact, looks like you'll be meeting him sooner than expected!" she says, rubbing her temples in slight pain. "After you do, let's share our precious reward, okay?" she adds.

Suddenly, in the blank skies of Void Imporia, the Astra's blue ribbon finally expires. The loose appendage rolls up, emitting the sound of a quiet bell. This soft chime rings across the entire surface of the blank island.

Followed by it, a weak shockwave that creates scratch marks and now, icy particles scatter all over the island. These particles were small and unnoticeable while other regions of the island produce cold crystal shards. Additionally, the metallic bits rose taller, as if they were blooming flowers. Those who fancied a blue color around their necks were nowhere to be found after this celestial event.

For a moment, the astral vibration steals all blue pigment from scarfs. The fast chime both distracted and disturbed Zyra from pronouncing anything. The airborne eruption returns back to its colorless state within moments as if nothing had happened.

Once the vibration settles down, Ophelia's body is nowhere to be found. Quickly afterward, Blank pokes his head towards the floating star. "The appendage!" he says to himself. "What was that!?" Zyra screams in fear. Dizzy, Zyra felt like she was going to faint out of the terrible tremble. "That is our signal to get the hell back to the arena!" Blank hassles.

"Heading back already?" Headless tiresomely asks. "Correct, we have a new set of monstrous obstacles to overcome." Blank starkly replies and heads back in the direction where they came from.

Headless and Blank proceed to leave the field that suddenly is full of icy shards poking out of the colorless sheets. "Zoriadia, we're running out of time!" he blurts with his hand cupped around his mouth. The gatekeeper swallows her words and meaninglessly follows the rest of the crew. She does, however, hold her blade resentfully. "W-What the hell is going on?" the lost gatekeeper mutters to herself.

Chapter VI:
Yikes! Intruder Alert!

Warnings of fateful encounters?

In the midst of the hollow Imporian land, the escapist continues to trudge fearfully. Volt and his robotic companion eventually reach the entrance of an abandoned monument that flourished in water colored patches. Unknowingly, a nearby figure has been ominously following their footsteps.

Volt, you've been running nonstop. Perhaps it's time to cool down a bit.

Forget about that! What the heck did I do to get targeted down by those doofs? That was mean, dude!

Analyzing internal voltage source to verify physical conditions...

Knock it off, Sympl. I won't rest until we get a safe shelter over our heads.

...So can you help me find a place instead of tickling me, please?

Error detected! Identified target approaching.

H-Huh!? Where!?

There you are, Champion! It's been an *eternity* since you left me alone all by myself! What's up?

Where did you... Erg, bug off, will ya?

Aw, are you not excited to see me again? Did I drop by at a bad time...?

Excited? You failed to tell me that weirdos are going to *hunt me down* for my stupid scarf!

Oops! Looks like I forgot to mention that part! Well, good job for doing your homework, Champion!

Forgot!? You can't just dump stuff onto me and forget the most important part!

Data dumping inappropriate files is wrong.

"Oh! That explains why you're mad! I must apologize for the inconvenience! I was just too shocked to learn that I had met the champion before anyone else!" Ophelia exclaims. Her genuine frown gets the best of Volt and makes him calm down a bit – but not enough to halt his hyperness. Sympl doesn't comprehend her gesture mainly because he can't see what is in front of his host. Yet, Sympl feels uncomfortable about her presence.

Volt takes a couple of silent moments to see her static position as he unsteadily exhales. "I just thought that was something you needed to clarify from the start... In fact, do you think there's anything worse than getting beaten up when home doesn't exist anymore?" Volt taunts. "Actually, yes. That's why we need to talk." She replies bluntly. Fidgety, Volt pauses his gestures and listens to what the prophet had to say.

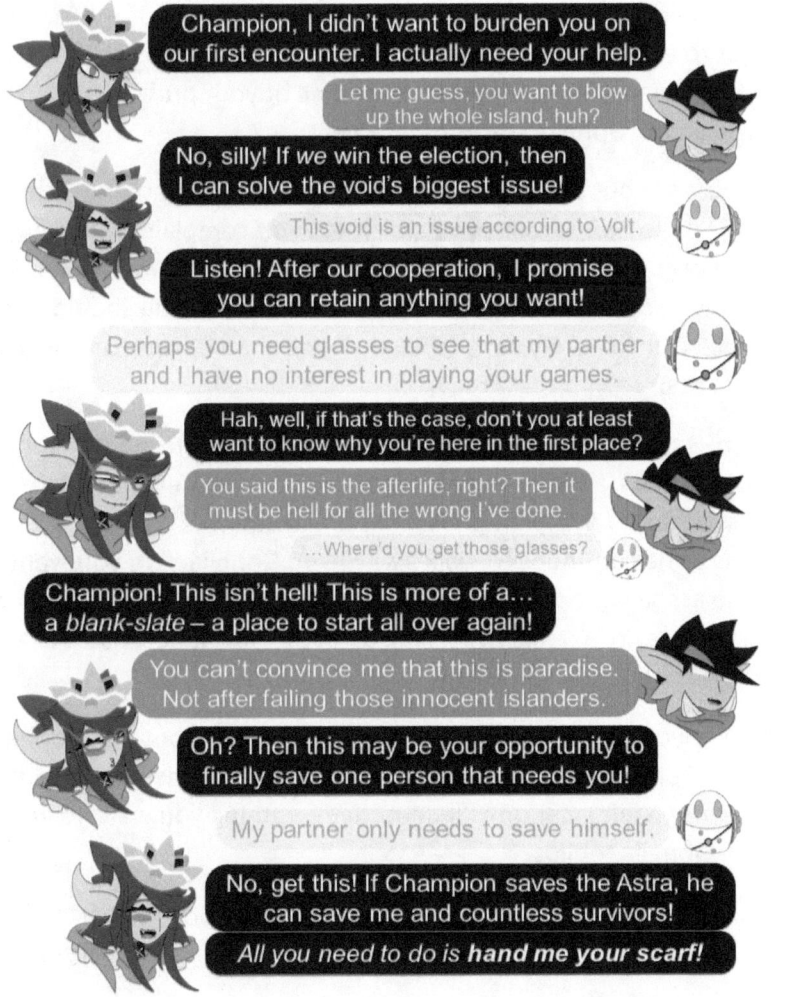

Champion, I didn't want to burden you on our first encounter. I actually need your help.

Let me guess, you want to blow up the whole island, huh?

No, silly! If *we* win the election, then I can solve the void's biggest issue!

This void is an issue according to Volt.

Listen! After our cooperation, I promise you can retain anything you want!

Perhaps you need glasses to see that my partner and I have no interest in playing your games.

Hah, well, if that's the case, don't you at least want to know why you're here in the first place?

You said this is the afterlife, right? Then it must be hell for all the wrong I've done.

...Where'd you get those glasses?

Champion! This isn't hell! This is more of a... a *blank-slate* – a place to start all over again!

You can't convince me that this is paradise. Not after failing those innocent islanders.

Oh? Then this may be your opportunity to finally save one person that needs you!

My partner only needs to save himself.

No, get this! If Champion saves the Astra, he can save me and countless survivors!

*All you need to do is **hand me your scarf!***

With the two staring down at each other without evident answers, Volt scoffs to break the silence. "You too, huh?" – "This scarf belongs to Volt and Sympl." his robotic backpack pitches in. "You just want to get this fabled 'pants of happiness,' wear it and call it a day." Volt goofs. "Well, it's for the benefit of everyone. Isn't that noble enough for—" Ophelia gets interrupted.

"Everyone? Who is everyone? Can't be the innocent islanders! Are you referring to the same punks that want to beat up a stranger for wearing some pink scarf?" Volt flabbergasts. "My beautiful champion, they are just racing to grab it for their own selfish reasons! "

"You don't *really* care about me either, Ophelia. You just want to use me like everyone else." Volt snaps. Ophelia frowns, "I would never want to hurt my beloved champion unless it was an emergency!" – "Then why did you forget to tell me how I'm a walking target?" Volt snaps back. "It's simple! Hand me a piece of your cloth and all of your problems will wash away over time!" Ophelia states defensively.

"Just get out of my way already. *Your* people are trying to hunt me down and I'm not going to let you stall me." Volt complains. She winces in return and breaks her silence, "You really think I don't care? Then take this warning! If you care about your safety and well-being, you should not enter that arena." Ophelia sadly says. "Exactly." Volt then begins to walk towards the arena area.

"H-Hey! I just said if you go there, you'll get in trouble!" Ophelia yelps with a genuinely shocked expression. "You are preventing us from hiding, aren't you?" Sympl queries. "C'mon, Sympl. We're wasting time." Volt warns as he continues to walk away from Ophelia. "Do you want to die there? The arena is a bad place for you, Champion!" – "I'm not here to fool around anymore. You're clearly telling us not to visit it because *it is* a safe place." Volt confidently spouts.

"Are you really that dumb? Do you not care about my prophetical warnings?" Ophelia hassles as she tries to catch up to the escaping duo. "Is that not enough information? I'll unearth everything you want to know! Just don't go!" Ophelia replies.

In style, Sympl bleeps loudly, "Loading keyword: 'Unearth...' Are you implying that there is something buried under our feet?" This freezes Volt in his tracks. Once again, Ophelia oddly winces, "That's not what I... Erg, for a talking backpack, you really compliment Champion's slow brain." she snarls disturbs the analyzing duo.

"At least Volt's brain has the ability to actively intake the flow of blood via his electro-heart. This therefore allows his neurons to properly function and comprehend the fact that you're an absolute oddball. Unlike your brain, which does not even operate since your heart does not show off signals of beating." Sympl speeches. "What...?" Volt whispers to himself. "She's braindead and cold-hearted." Sympl replies. "Uh... Are you calling her a zombie?" Volt quietly murmurs to Sympl.

"How dare you say that! You're the cold-hearted parasite here, Sympl! You're not giving me a chance talk to my champion!" Ophelia adds. "In conclusion, there is no necessity to continue listening to your data dumps." Sympl raspberries, indirectly forcing Volt to walk away from her. Ophelia then rushes towards the fleeing champion one last time.

"Champion! Stop playing hard to get already! It's really rude when you don't pay attention to yours truly!" Ophelia loftily says. "Now, do you want to help me stop poor Astra from dying and save countless victims?" Her serious stares forces Volt to look away somehow. How could the Imporian reluctantly avoid dodging this question? It was an obvious opportunity to prove his worth as a gatekeeper – or so he initially thought.

Ophelia's serious stare evolves into a glare. "...Or are you going to listen to that bothersome backpack?" Ophelia piques once more. Sympl emits his unusual beeping sounds, "Master Volt, permission to use tactical cable arms?" The robotic companion raises its electrical cables at an intimidating pose. "Sympl, enough already." Volt calmly yet gloomily states.

Upon seeing how the robotic companion eases up on command, Ophelia tensely holds her stance in front of Volt. Between the baffled Imporian and the arena, the prophet's blocking body persistently wedges herself onto his tracks. Her concerns appear honest – specifically with her big red winking eye darting into Volt's soul. "...Are you going to keep on ignoring me?" she adds with sorrow. To this, he silently passes by her blockade. Volt continues to trudge towards the arena.

"I'm not going to let my guard down again..." Volt mumbles before disappearing into the direction of the forsaken arena. Once he manages to escape from the prophet's line of vision, Ophelia releases a repressive exhale to herself.

Hastily, Volt flees into the chiseled monument. The escaping duo frantically scans the vast arena. The sheer colossal size of the arena makes Volt feel like a spec of dirt. As he wonders in awe, Sympl flares another warning alarm.

Another error detected! Unidentified lifeforce nearby!

I thought this place was empty!

Target is directly in front of you, Volt.

I don't... I don't see anyone. Hold on! Are you talking about my front or back?

That egg...

There's no mistaking it!

Orientation is indeed incorrect. Approaching targets approaching from this unit's left side.

T-Targets!? You mean the doofs again?

Negative, "doofs" do not wear masks.

Hearing the robot's digital voice box say such words makes Volt evermore jumpy. He rotates his body to distantly see a gang of figures walking towards the direction of the arena. The idea of encountering more strangers who have an interest in his scarf deeply scares him.

Exiting through the arena's arches would only leave him vulnerable in the void. Realizing that the outsiders could catch him, Volt impulsively springs onto the arena's bleachers. He sprints behind one of the empty columns in an attempt to hide his body from the approaching gang. Upon doing so, the duo heard rattling.

Viola slides herself away from the column she hid at. The puppet lady then desperately skips down towards the center of the arena. She looks out of the arches to see Blank and his henchmen returning to their home base. She quickly dashes towards them, "Mister Blank! *Void master* detected!" the lady outcries.

"Where?" Blank grits thoughtlessly. Viola jets her claw at the direction of Volt's hiding spot, allowing for Blank to react. The masked leader sprints at Viola's implied direction with his arms transforming into the pin shape. Zyra and Headless gawk at their leader's speed. Blank then relentlessly plants his sharp pinned arm into the column, shattering it like glass. Sympl's reactive cable arms were able to push Volt away on time.

"The hell!?" Blank screeches once his invisible eyes connect with Volt's figure. Given Volt's unusual physique, the masked leader freezes his movement for a second. On the other hand, the Imporian did not waste a second staying still – Volt bounces out of danger. Repositioned between bleachers and the center of the arena, he learns that he is somewhat surrounded.

Stuck with his pinned arm grounded in cement, Blank gleams at the intruder. Grazing at his vibrant velvet scarf, sharp ears, and erected fangs, Blank concludes that Volt must be the monster that the prophet had previously mentioned. "Velvet scarfer! You've invaded the wrong property!" Blank aggressively barks.

Volt glances around the arena for an escape route only to freeze upon laying his eyes on one of the Aphotic members. Zyra exerts her usual cold expression but flinches once she sees how Volt emits familiarity. Every muscle in her body tenses up as she could only stare at the monstrous figure.

With his eyes locked at Zyra, Volt loses focus on his own movement. Sympl's cable arms sweep his feet, forcing Volt to move towards any exiting arch. Headless dashes towards Volt with a knife in his palms. Headless strikes without fear, but before landing any cuts, Sympl's cable arms whip the wrist of the offender.

The steel of the knife hits the ground, ringing a quiet metallic impact. Immediately, Headless continues to combat against the Imporian with a fury of punches and kicks. Sympl blocks these attacks with more fast-paced whipping. Volt uses the small window opportunity to push Headless into the ground and then jolts towards the exiting arch.

Blank finally unshackles his pinned arms from the cement of the cracked column. Free from the clutches of the cement, the masked man sprints straight at Volt and drags his pins across the ground. The floor raspingly screeches since dragging the pins directly sharpened its edges. Blank nears Volt and relentlessly attempts to stab him.

With the assistance of Sympl's tactical wires, Volt barely dodges the darting pins. In one instance, Volt uses his palms to catch the polished pin.

Blank slides his arm away, leaving red marks over Volt's palms. Having the red mark drip over the velvet scarf heats up Volt's body for a split second. This dripping red paint also spreads onto some of Sympl's robotic cables. Like a burning sensation, the Imporian briefly yelps in pain and continues to fend off Blank's relentless swings.

During this time, Headless picks up his knife and hammers his way towards Volt. All of the flaps that Sympl had controlled flew in multiple directions in an attempt to defend his partner from any serious damage. "Sympl is overheating!" the robotic voice alarms while it fences off against the two Aphotic members.

Being stranded in the middle of the duel, Volt defensively places his arms over his head. Afterall, he had absolutely no control of Sympl's tactical wires – the only thing he could do is escape; a fleet he struggles with. Despite Sympl's swift retaliation, Volt panics over the idea of Sympl's systems failing. "Overheating!?" Volt yelps after being shocked with the paint-like burn.

From the distance, Zyra gazes at the struggling intruder. Her throat gets dry and sweat trickles at the back of her neck. The similarity of the monstrous figure she stares at continues to haunt her. Was it the shoulder pads of the gatekeeper that reminded her of Draw's struggle? Or more importantly, did she see the face of a friend in pain?

Zyra silently gulps then charges at the fight with her sword in the air. "Move!" she impulsively bellows. Hearing her announcement, Blank and Headless halt their vicious attacks for a short-lived moment. She then takes a small leap, holding out the handle of her blade towards Volt.

Reactively, Sympl latches onto the handle of her weapon and with strength only, aggressively flips her over. With enough space to squeeze himself out of his surroundings, Volt drags himself towards an arch of the arena. The panting Imporian manages to escape the deadly monument but is immediately chased down by Headless, who was able to reclaim its knife.

The masked leader surveys the arena's conditions. He spots Viola hiding behind one of the arena's broken columns and Zyra laying on the floor. With an angry grit written on his face, Blank proceeds to approach the floored Zyra.

Blank almost rips Zyra's arm off when lifting her. He then follows a trail of red liquid that the escapist left behind. Away by a few metrics, Zyra catches up and joins the hot chase. It only took moments before Volt found himself getting chased by the persistent group of hunters known as Aphotic.

"Hang in there, buddy!" Volt pants as he feels the robot heating up.

Chapter VII:
Isothermal Relentlessness

When will enough be enough?

In his hasty runaway, the escapist continues to lock his vision on the group that pursued him. He peaks ahead of himself only to find vague figures in the distance. "Error detected! Targets known as "doofs" are in approaching radius." the warm robotic backpack weakly states.

Once the figure's faces were visible, Volt dreadfully halts. The Imporian turns his head around to see how Aphotic was catching up. With his path blocked by Reza and her comrades, Volt found himself surrounded.

Is that magenta dude again?

Not the doofs again...
Please, get out of my way!

Nobody move a muscle!

You brought hunters!?

They followed me here!

Pfft, Hunters? That's "Leader of Aphotic" to you. Learn how to address your superiors, blueberry.

Aphotic!? You're the ones that are preying on innocent people! Why would you do such a thing!?

Scavenging scarves is required to liberate this eternal dread. Get out of my damn way or perish.

All of this for a stupid scarf?

Under no conditions shall you ever hurt anyone ever again! Your tyranny ends now!

In the middle of his adversaries, the magenta target glares at those who have wanted to hunt him down for his scarf. Tension fills the air since both parties face off each other down with one goal in mind – who shall claim their target?

76

The escapist and his overheating robotic backpack flee the scene without hesitancy. In his escape, the remains of a leafless forest could faintly be seen off the horizon. Volt commits to the forest as his last resort for shelter.

With Volt zapping himself out of the crowd, every person tensely spreads out. While everyone takes a precautious footstep towards their opponents, Blank leaps over to the fleeing Imporian. Automatically, Hassen whacks his staff at Blank, triggering the clash between the two parties.

Blank counter-swings his razor-sharp pin-arms to divide the staff into splinters. Weaponless, Hassen crosses his arms to guard his body as Allena swings in to defend Hassen. The lady's immense speed and precision allows her to hit Blank's torso, knocking him onto the ground.

Thoughtlessly, Allena reaches her hands out to Blank's scarf. Before she could attempt to latch her hands onto the leader's cloth, Headless sprints and kicks Allena out of Blank's grasp. The force of the kick sends the lady dynamically rolling across the cold floors. With no hesitation, Headless chases the sliding lady with his knife out.

Reza's eyes lit up upon seeing the pocket knife. She tries to dash towards her fallen comrade only to be blocked by Zyra's sword. The gatekeeper cynically stares at the worried guardian. She elevates her sword's tip to reach the edge of Reza's neck. Out of remorse, Zyra points her blade upwards. "S-Stop this…" Reza mutters under her breath.

"For your own safety, do not move…" Zyra whispers. The gatekeeper remains frozen and does not take any further action. At Reza's peripheral vision, she witnesses Headless cutting Allena's scarf out of her neck. Freed from the wrapped cloth, Allena screams at the top of her lungs as she begins to painfully evaporate into thin air.

Alerted at the devastating screeching, Hassen pelts parts of his broken staff at Headless. Headless then feels the spikey shards piercing through his protective wool. These shards cause him to flinch for mere moments. In the span of seconds, Hassen runs towards the prickled Aphotic member only to feel agonizing pain.

From the ground, Blank had stabbed his lengthy pin-arm into Hassen's back. Not only did this cause the bulky guardian to freeze in sheer pain, but the masked leader's arm drips more of its red liquids. Blank then ferociously slides his arm up to Hassen's neck, creating a massive flesh wound and more importantly, snapping his scarf out of his neck.

The large body wordlessly falls onto the ground. Spurs of hot particles quickly left his massive body. The masked leader then marks another tally on his faceplate with the fresh red liquid his arms dripped. Nauseous from seeing her comrade nearly get ripped in half, Reza backs away from Zyra's blockade. With her every muscle trembling, Reza releases a loud cry and recklessly swings her metallic staff in an attempt to fight back.

Zyra dodges this, which allows Reza to impulsively make her way to the evaporating bodies with the hopes of saving them somehow. "Stop!" Zyra yells at Reza only for her words to be rendered useless. Headless stops plucking various amounts of wooden shards once he spots Reza running at Blank. The Aphotic member instantly makes a mad dash with his knife aimed at her. Aware of the nearby target, Reza spins herself and violently swings her gigantic paintbrush at Headless, fracturing his torso and forcing him to fly.

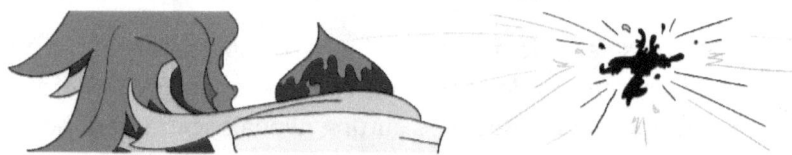

The airborne henchman fades into thin air like a firework. Wondering how such force was possible, Blank realizes that his comrade's scarf was attached to the rim of Reza's paintbrush. Finally, Reza reaches Blank and relentlessly swings her brush at Blank. Seeing this from a mile away, Blank comically dodges all of her flails and even taunts her with a chuckle.

As the fear-induced Reza continues to blindly attack Blank, he reverts his pins back into his normal hands then to holds them up as if he were surrendering. Distracted by the leader's raised palms, Reza slows down the pacing of her swings. Suddenly, Blank's palms burst into pins again, blowing Reza's weapon away from her and flooring her in the process.

Blank releases a subtle snicker. "Did you really think you could stop me with that toothbrush?" Between Blank's cocky attitude, Reza's frozen state, and the heat of the evaporating comrades, insanity brews into Zyra's mind. Blank raises his pin arm and right before the finishing blow lands on Reza's crown, Zyra knocks over Reza and swings her stone-like sword back at Blank's crashing pin.

The clash between the red-scarves intensifies.

Grinding his pin again Zyra's sword, Blank grits, "Get the hell out of my way…!" Upon pushing him away, she waves her hand signaling a break. "Are you that stupid!?" Zyra desperately pants for air. As she gasps for air, Reza gradually jitters into escaping the scene yet struggles mustering up the energy to do so.

"Are you forgetting about friendly fire!?" Zyra cries out. Blank recoils upon hearing the reminder — had he harmed anyone with a red scarf, his candidacy for the election would be terminated, right? Blank hesitates to back off only to finally connect the dots. He cracks an invisible sweat upon realizing his mistake. He was still stiff and on guard for any possible subtle movements.

Perhaps it was the way how Reza's floored body expressed gentleness. Perhaps it was her discolored shoulder and chest pad. Maybe it the roaring steam of the nearby evaporating bodies. It could've easily been her teary and red-painted face. But Zyra could not bare to see a reflection of herself — a weak body on the ground, unable to escape a mighty inferno. If it wasn't for her savior, she would never have been saved, fostered and grown as a noble gatekeeper. Zyra did not want more chaos — she craved reason.

80

How ungrateful. You should be *thrilled* to get rid of a traitor like him.

You're a sick freak! How dare you take away the life of another so freely!? You're the nastiest person I know!

I'm doing the fattest favor you could ever fathom, blueberry.

Zyra's cold stare pierces through the leader's thick mask. Whimpering in both shame and fear, Reza does not hassle to use this opportunity to flee the scene. As she shamefacedly cowards away from Aphotic's escape, she snatches her hefty paintbrush before disappearing from their sight. Reza successfully runs away with tears flooding her face.

Zyra releases a silent sigh, "Let go of your distractions! Don't we have a mission to finish?" Zyra questions as she sees Reza's figure faintly disappearing towards the horizon of the void. Blank scuffs in embarrassment, "Stop the election..."

Confirming her theory about Aphotic's reasoning gave Zyra a sense of relief. With her itchy nose finally being scratched, Zyra's inner thoughts had calmed down. However, Blank cracks a very small, unnoticeable smirk. "Stop the election..." Blank sinisterly repeats.

"...Let's stop wasting time. Time to end happiness." Blank grazes. The remaining duo of Aphotic nod at each other and then race towards the nearby forest. They could barely catch a glimpse of Volt's velvet scarf fading into the forest. Dreary and full of dark water-color patches, Blank recklessly submerges himself into the woods. Spikey branches blocked any space to freely roam through the area.

Chapter VIII:
Severed Scarves

How elastic are plastic friends?

Upon carelessly jogging through the woods, Blank gets a small piece of his clothing entangled by the sharp branches. Annoyed, he uses his pin-arms to cut away the thick twigs. Once dead branches hit the floor, the masked leader notes other pieces of cloth tethered in the woods.

"Zoriadia! Hold on! These branches aren't meant for speeding." Blank shouts. His words do not resonate with Zyra since she was too busy plowing through the mazy forest. Blank grits to himself and slowly cuts down branches to catch up. "I said hold up!" the leader fiercely shouts. His voice echoes through the forest and descends into a muted mumble.

In the meantime, Volt continues to rattle through the spikey forest with ease thanks to Sympl's cables dodging all chunks of wood. Despite Sympl's automated assistance and a safe run through the woods, Volt's heart was still pounding from the battle's tension. "C'mon, c'mon…!" Volt murmurs to himself.

Swinging her sword relentlessly, Zyra chops all obstacles in her path at an incredible speed. With each slice, she madly groans given that the deeper she got, the more branches appeared. In her destructive run, she eventually locks a glimpse of the velvet scarf she was chasing for.

Suddenly, Zyra feels a slight yank on her neck. Her scarf had been restrained by a hanging branch. In an attempt to cut the branch loose, the edge of her blade also gets stuck. Trapped, she struggles to break free but feels the wrapped cloth loosening around her neck.

A huge crater was tucked in at the center of the forest. Conveniently, as Volt reaches the crater, Sympl barely sees Zyra's body reaching the edge of the forest. "Error detected!" the robotic backpack spouts. Catching his attention, Volt rotates to see what the robotic had detected. "Ignore the enemy, Sympl. We got places to be." Volt coldly replies.

Zyra continues to hassle and groan in her imprisoned position. Despite all her efforts, she begins to feel the branches prickling against her skin. "Stop running away, coward!" Zyra painfully bellows.

"Coward!?" Volt replies. The pure anger he felt flared throughout Sympl, emitting bits of electrical sparks out of his back. The sparkling discharge intimidates the trapped gatekeeper. In atrocious fear, she quickly grows timid to the point where she regrets chasing the monstrous Imporian. Yet, her undying curiosity begs her to ask the beast about the fate of her friend. "What did you do to Thevenin!?" Zyra timorously shouts.

Volt stops and directs himself towards Zyra. A wave of nostalgia hits hit him hard, yet his bitterness prevents him from lasering his eyes onto her. His nightmares were confirmed; it was Zyra in the flesh. He takes a deep breath and uneasily shutters. "Zyra..." Volt says with a fragile tone.

Hearing his uneasy voice alerted the trapped gatekeeper. She jeers for a moment only to connect the dots. "No way... Y-You actually are Thevenin, aren't you...?" Zyra hesitantly questions. "Duh, I ended up getting a pretty-pink makeover. Do you like it? Although, I think I need a haircut soon..." the Imporian sarcastically replies.

Hearing Thevenin's usual silly attitude eases her tension. She gets enlightened and takes a deep sigh of relief. "My goodness... You have no idea how badly I need a friend right now..." she awkwardly says with a soft smile.

"Friends? Pfft, we're not friends after what you've done." Volt snaps, glaring into Zyra's surprised eyes. Zyra's heart sinks. Hearing her once silly friend act suddenly serious at an elongated reunion disturbs her. Even with the warmth of her skin-protector, she couldn't help but feel chills upon hearing his deep voice.

"When I woke up, I quickly became a prisoner of my own thoughts in that sinkhole." he monologued. Fully focused as his words, Zyra disregards struggling in her trapped position. "Not only did you imprison me, but now that I'm free, you're also trying to beat me up – *again*." Volt states miserably. "The hell? I would never in a million years imprison you!"

Zyra snaps back. "What's wrong with you!?" she adds with a more aggressive tone.

"Where did you leave me to die, Zyra?" Volt coldly asks. "Where did you leave me before that damn hatchening destroyed our island?" he adds.

It took a couple of absolute silent moment for Zyra to realize what her 'supposed' friend is referring to about. Upon connecting even more dots, her expression twists from one of ponder to utter disbelief. "...No, that was not the intention, Thevenin."

"Intention, huh? You want to talk about intentions? Then tell me if you remember the intention behind that sword." Volt remarks while gazing at Zyra's stone-like sword. "...It was intended to be used as a weapon, right?" Zyra sheepishly replies as she begins to struggle with eye contact.

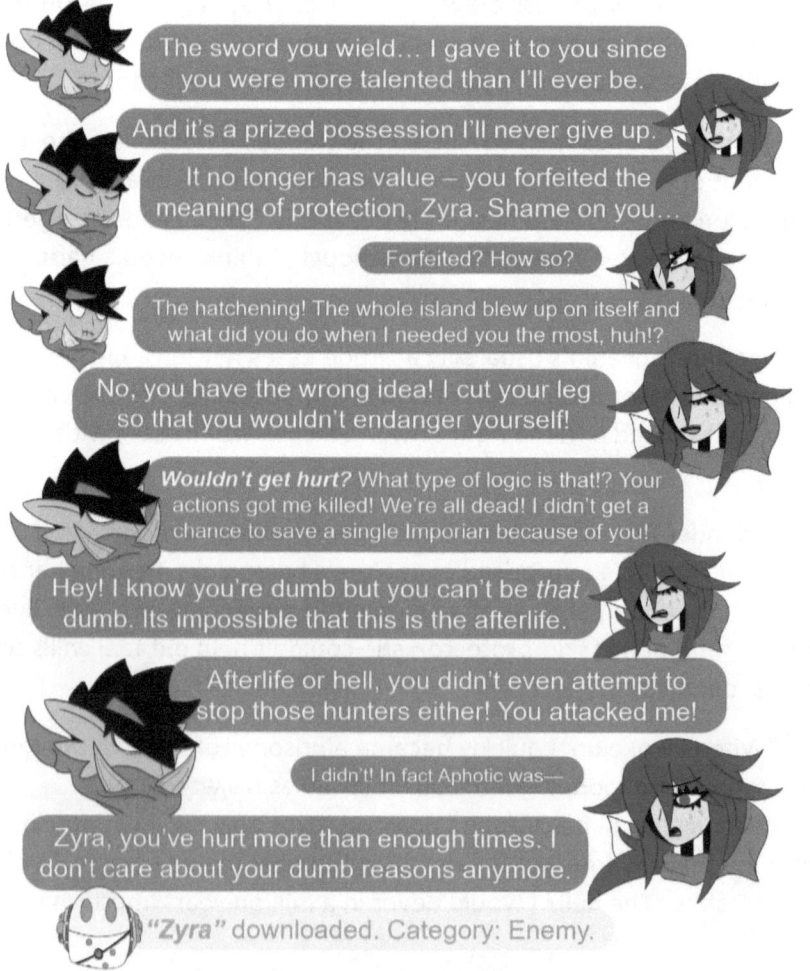

The sword you wield... I gave it to you since you were more talented than I'll ever be.

And it's a prized possession I'll never give up.

It no longer has value — you forfeited the meaning of protection, Zyra. Shame on you...

Forfeited? How so?

The hatchening! The whole island blew up on itself and what did you do when I needed you the most, huh!?

No, you have the wrong idea! I cut your leg so that you wouldn't endanger yourself!

Wouldn't get hurt? What type of logic is that!? Your actions got me killed! We're all dead! I didn't get a chance to save a single Imporian because of you!

Hey! I know you're dumb but you can't be *that* dumb. Its impossible that this is the afterlife.

Afterlife or hell, you didn't even attempt to stop those hunters either! You attacked me!

I didn't! In fact Aphotic was—

Zyra, you've hurt more than enough times. I don't care about your dumb reasons anymore.

"Zyra" downloaded. Category: Enemy.

Volt's grudge on his once loyal friend continues to cultivate.

"I wish I never gave you a chance." Volt spoke. His cold words pierced Zyra's heart in half. "You got in my way that one night and I can't help but think things would've been way different if I chose someone else." Volt eerily approaches Zyra. His overwhelmingly towering stature strikes fear towards Zyra. "G-Get it through your thick skull, Thev! I'm not here to hurt you!" Zyra lashes out as both tears and cold sweat commence to drip from her petrified face.

Out of irritation, Volt reaches his hand out and grabs her red scarf.

He slowly pulls the bleeding cloth out of her neck. Zyra's sweating floods her pale face. After pulling her scarf a bit, he notices that he'll need to violently yank the cloth since it was entangled by the sharp branches. Here, Volt notices the texture and other details of her scarf. With the lengthy wool in his palms, he exerts a silent sigh.

"...This is stupid." Volt says in defeat as he ultimately releases her loose scarf from his harsh grip. "You want my scarf like everyone else, but I just don't get the thrill behind these things." Volt states in disgust. "You really think this is fun? Tugging on someone's scarf? Pfft, how childish." he adds upon giving her a dark stare.

Zyra's heartrate slows down upon feeling the slight tugging diminish into nothing. She still couldn't help her frozen state and continues to stressfully shiver facial fluids.

"After all I've done for you, I can't believe you really don't give a damn. Looks like the gatekeepers were right about you after all." Volt says as he lavishly turns his back at her. "Error detected!" Sympl pitches upon refacing the trapped lady. The robotic tactical cables fly towards the air and dramatically spark up. "Sympl, let's get out of here." Volt calmly says as his backpacking companion refuses to tie away its sparkling tentacles.

Regardless of all the heartbeat-skipping moments Zyra took in, she nods rapidly, "This is a misunderstanding! I-I'm not done with you!" Zyra bellows. "I am, troublemaker." Volt replies. "T-Thevenin!" Zyra shouts reluctantly while Volt simply walks away further into the forest.

With his hollow expression, Volt puffs his chest. "Thevenin died when you broke his heart." the monstrous, robotic-backpacking, velvet-scarf wearer remorsefully stated. Volt refused to look back and he abandons Zyra in her strangled position.

Chapter IX:
A Wishful Stance

Only your truest allies can help you reach your goals...

The grimy forest remains silent. Volt continues to trudge out of the woods to ensure a great distance from Zyra – a true traitor. Once he visually disappears from her sight, his robotic companion beings to emit discreet beeping.

"Volt, what do you plan to do now?" the backpacking robot questions. The escapist silently continues to trudge, ignorantly avoiding his companion's queries. "Perhaps we should attempt to discover a solution to return to your home island, Imporia. Does that not sound pleasant to you?" Once again, the deprived Imporian remains silent upon hearing the chattering robot.

"Or how about we investigate the materialistic properties of the Astra? Perhaps then we can analyze and replicate—" before Sympl could finish his speech, Volt coldly barks back, "Stop it." The wood-roaming Imporian halts his footsteps. "There is no 'going home,' and frankly, there's no point in doing so." Volt states in monotone.

Before Sympl could try to wedge an opinion, the robot senses yet another approaching individual, resulting in it to outcry its signature alarm. "Error detected!" the robotic device erupts. Hearing the warning flare up only made Volt wince his eyes annoyingly. The Imporian scans and searches for anything that moved and eventually spotted the figure.

"Speaking of the devil..." he mutters to himself. The duo spot Ophelia toying around with sharp tree branches. She is seen yanking branches that could fit in a sachet that matches her outfit. The odd lady then catches a glimpse of the duo and then poses. Excited, she briefly jumps in joy before slamming the traveling duo with her unusual prompts.

Champion! Looks like you found me! Does that mean I'm 'it?'

I'm curious to how you keep appearing out of nowhere...

You really want to play, huh? It'd be really fun to see you close your eyes permanently.

Excuse me...? Is hide'n'seek too much to bare? How about a different game?

Stop being such a stupid child. I'm not here to play your dumb games, you creepy stalker.

Oh you *really* don't want to play anymore...

The Imporian gives a spiteful glance at the impish lady. "Why don't we take it easy now?" Ophelia begins to speak. With a cold expression and arms crossed, Volt squints his eyes in preparation for hearing her petty speech. "It's really impressive how you are wearing the champion's scarf so proudly!" she adds with a snicker.

"I'm a bit surprised you're still in one piece! Afterall, I told you that something really bad was going to happen, remember?" Ophelia teases. With a stoic expression, Volt doesn't attempt to reply. "...Say! Since when did your fangs get longer? I didn't know those sharp bad boys could grow!" She goofily comments as the unflinching duo statically stood still.

"O-Oh! Don't worry! Since we're both here, alone, deep in the woods, *where no one will ever find out what could possibly happen,* I can finally unearth what you need to know!" Ophelia playfully teases with a quick wink. Volt's eerie silence begins to poke into Ophelia's mentality.

"Freak..." Volt sarcastically whispers while rolling his imaginary pupils, interrupting her confounded sob story. "Eh? I was just going to... Look, you will be granted another chance at happiness if you—!" – "Liar." Volt blurts. "This scarf is making me absolutely miserable." Volt adds. He churns his neck away from the disturbed prophet.

Ophelia's impish ears spike-up. "How dare you mock the election and the velvet scarf!" Ophelia yelps. Yet again, Volt and Sympl fail to flinch to Ophelia's change of tone. "I'm disappointed in you, Champion! If you don't desire to win another chance at happiness after everything you've been through, then you clearly don't deserve to wear that scarf!" Ophelia angrily says before reaching out her hand towards Volt's scarf.

Sympl's optical lens warmly radiates a red flashing light and warns his companion, "Battle mode, on!" As Sympl's wires latch onto the scarf's flaps, the wires forcefully snap Ophelia's lustrous claws.

Snap!

Instantly, a loud flick and pained cry echo through the woods. The impish lady softly gropes her wrist to ease the flickering agony. She shakes at the searing robotic cables and tucks her now cracked claws with her other sleeve. Her sincere expression transforms into an unbelievable look – shocked as if a child been punished by its mother. Volt emotionlessly stares down at the scared prophet.

With a delayed reaction, Volt cringes at himself for allowing such violence but resumes to exert a cold expression. In silence, Sympl raises the cables in the air, ready to strike at Ophelia once again. Induced in fear, she asks, "…W-Why do you wish to keep wearing it if it is so fruitless to you?"

"I am *not* your champion." The furious Imporian demandingly declares, striking terror towards Ophelia.

The speechless lady silently gulps to herself and hesitantly takes a step away. The vicious duo silently glares at the pained prophet before barging into another direction. Volt walks away to more unknown regions only for Ophelia to spew "You really are a monster…" With Volt's back facing her, Sympl releases a raspberry before disappearing into the collection of towering trees.

. . .

Meanwhile, Reza frantically rushes back in the same direction where she came from. She reaches the safe perimeters of the fort only to heavily drop onto the ground. Reza volumetrically mourns over the loss of her comrades as she rapidly gasps for air. Her uncontrollable sobbing alerted Grant and Amphy who were already on their way to welcome her back. Seeing her terrified state roiled their stomachs.

Upon asking what had happened, her reply was too sloppy to be understood. Grant simply empathizes with her by leaning over. He reaches his hand out, ready to pat her, but recalls her backlashing at him for not having the permission to touch her in any way. To this, he quietly retracts his hand and observes her cry.

Under Reza's ocean of snot and tears were shattered expectations of comfort. How could an older gentleman ever promise her safety? What did she expect when savaging for leftovers in a void jam-packed with violence? These thoughts were mere fantasies that covered all of her recent trauma.

The inaudible failure of a collector tries to explain what had occurred when she encountered Aphotic. This time her voice resides more passionate anger than the drowned-out sorrow she spoke. Amphy inconsiderately wraps his arms around his depressed guardian. His soft hug eases her up a bit, "Reza! It's going to be okay!" the hopeful boy comforts. During the sibling's seek of relief, Grant's attention was focused on the yellow scarf that wrangled in Reza's paintbrush.

In one of Reza's slurred words, Grant hears the guardian mention "Hu-hunters..." It didn't take any time for the elder to draw a conclusion on what had occurred. However, his thoughts aimed more to how he could help. Upon gently asking her to be clearer, Reza tragically fails to compose herself. The anxious elder then gazes at a faint trail of red water-colored patches Reza had involuntarily dragged with her.

Grant's eyes were more than alerted; whatever had happened can be traced back into the fort where they were all hiding. "A trail...?" he mutters to himself. "If we don't move..." he jumbles in silence. Grant then scans the fort area and solidifies his thought process on what to do next. "...No, we're going to have to put an end to all of these rascals." the determined elder silently declares to himself.

Left behind in the doomed forest, Zyra gives up on undoing herself from her trapped position. Emotionally exhausted, the gatekeeper rests her teary eyes. Alone, she reflects what her actions had led to.

Wandering in the shady woods, Ophelia finds herself visiting the center of the forsaken forest. Here, she barely spots a dim body embedded in the murky group of wooden trunks. She takes a few moments to analyze how Zyra could've trapped herself given her funky position. The prophet then takes a deep breath and calmly approaches Zyra. "Oh...?" Ophelia whispers to herself.

Upon getting up close and personal, the prophet softly strokes her smooth, undamaged claws over the gatekeeper's hair. Startled, the gatekeeper recoils her head against Ophelia's grab. "Y-You!" Zyra screeches as Ophelia hushes her. "Shh... relax, relax. We've both had long days, haven't we?" As difficult as it was to move, Zyra resists from Ophelia's sudden petting.

"This is so exciting though! I finally get to have one-on-one time with you! You were asking all types of questions with Blanky-poo, no?" Ophelia giggles as Zyra continues her struggle fest. "Yet... You were just doing you were told to do, weren't you?" Ophelia questions calmly.

Zyra doesn't sit well with the fact that the prophet of all people just happens to casually approach and pet her hair. However, with the soothing strokes of her polish claws and Ophelia's genuine tone, Zyra somehow ends up relaxing to an extent. This petting reminds her of a fond time she had with a certain friend.

92

Ophelia then proceeds to meticulously chop down the branches that had trapped Zyra with her functioning claws. Once she had been freed, Ophelia pulls out a red cloth from her sleeve and asks for Zyra to stay still. Within moments, she had been knitting Zyra's scratched-up scarf with small razor-sharp twigs stored in her hood-like sachet.

"All patched up!" the prophet cheerfully says after Zyra notes that her scarf had been knitted into a mended condition.

I'm in love with your reckless attitude! But you should really be aware of your environment, y'know?

If you want to win the election so badly, then why are you wasting time patching me up?

The same reason why I've been bugging everyone wearing red! We need to collaborate and end this together!

...You were right about the monster.

My predictions never fail, dear. It's like a voice in my head. In fact, it keeps telling me what needs to be done.

Is that what's telling you how to win the election? Getting rid of the monster and taking his scarf?

Definitely. I'm not qualified to tackle such a beast. However, the voice keeps telling me that the one who wears red does.

And what does that lousy scarf do again?

Winner of the election wins another chance at happiness! Don't worry, if *we* win, I promise to *share* our rewards!

"I still don't know what any of that means..." Zyra confesses. The gatekeeper assumes that such an opportunity would permit her to live her wildest fantasies. Yet, her imagination gets hazy – could a 'troublemaker' like herself qualify for such a dream? Her mind boggles with a faint dream she had once envisioned.

Abruptly, Ophelia quickly flinches in burning pain. The prophet indirectly reveals her pair of cracked claws to Zyra. "That looks like it hurts..." Zyra comments. "Oh this? Y-Yeah, that's what happens when a poor defenseless little lady like me tries to work alone." Ophelia giggles crudely.

"...Anyway, another chance at happiness means exactly what you think it does." Ophelia adds with a solemn tone.

"I never had a proper chance to actually explain it, but another chance at happiness is a v—" Ophelia starts before hearing large rustling. Rustling from behind the gatekeeper grew louder. "Zoraidia!" Blank's voice dimly bellows. The two can hear the masked man desperately cutting the thick branches to safely make his way to Zyra.

"Bah, it's the party-pooper. Looks like if I stick here any longer, I'll get in some trouble. Besides, we wouldn't want our friend Blank to assume naughty things, would we?" Ophelia teasingly says. "Wait!" Zyra cries out. As Blank gradually drew closer, Ophelia's anxiety kicked in.

"Enough with the hint dropping!" Zyra continues to speak. "If you're so keen on getting help, you're going to need to tell me what the point of winning this entire election is about." Zyra demands. "...It's about preventing Ophelia from trapping us here." Blank's voice stated as he arrives. His blood-red pins had tons of splinters attached to them and his vest was severely scratched up.

"Blanky-poo!" Ophelia surprisingly says with subtle nervousness in her voice. "You're as stern as ever!" she titters around his entrance. "You touched Zoriadia, didn't you?" Blank stressfully questions. Ophelia's nervousness was wiped away from her uncontrollable giggling.

"Assuming naughty things already? We just bonded a little!" Ophelia replies as she attempts to contain her vile snickering. "Screw you and your dirty claws, Ophelia." Blank snaps only to examine her broken claws from afar. "Well, your wish is partially true..." Ophelia teasingly says as she flaunts her broken left hand.

"Trapping is the wrong word, Blank. It's everlasting freedom if anything." she tacks onto the conversation. "So, can we finally agree to stop fooling around and stop our monster together?" Ophelia sassily questions. "Aphotic exists to destroy your ideals, Ophelia – I'll never help you." Blank stomps. "Whether you like it or not, we need to mutually help each other to get that scarf." she confidently replies.

I would've loved to see you strangle me!

But that's okay! You're smart enough to know by now that it'll get you all hot and sweaty! Exciting, right?

Are you always this flirty?

Suggestive as always, Ophelia! Why don't I swap colors right now and legally slice you apart, huh?

Wow! I didn't think a criminal could also be a law-abiding citizen! Very impressive, Blanky-poo!

But if you are that focused on stopping me, its best for you to prioritize our monstrous problem!

I don't think Blank really has intentions to help you out...

Pfft, nothing you'll ever say is going to convince me to help your sorry-ass.

No matter what you plan, do or say, the results are already in Blanky-poo. It's just a matter of time.

The most beautiful part of all of this is that at the end of the road, you are always going to need me.

What do you precisely plan on doing if you win the election?

With another chance at happiness, I can finally save Astra from dying.

Hah! You plan on *freezing time!?* Screw that! Astra needs to die for us to all of us to escape this void.

95

"It's the perfect loophole to living forever and never facing death again! What's not to love about it? Save Astra, save the void, live forever!" Ophelia triumphantly speaks. She then glances at Blank hysterically, "Oh! That's right! It may offend you since you seem not to value life as much." Ophelia teases. The prophet then peacefully glances at Zyra. "I trust that our gatekeeper will know how to save us from the monster." Ophelia adds.

"Hah, 'ours' my ass!" Blank outcries as his hot glowing pin-arms aim to strike down the prophet. "Blanky-poo, your memory is failing you again! You need to remember that we share the same color! Hit me and you'll evaporate with me." Ophelia leverages with a wink. Boiling in anger, Blank glances over to Zyra to see serenity in her expression. It was Zyra who also reminded him to calm down around those who wore a red scarf.

"You and blueberry... You're really narrowing my options." Blank grits. "Now since we're on the same page, why don't we all get the velvet scarf? After all, that monster has multiple appendages so we could even share the victory!" Ophelia cheers. Blank suddenly pushes her away, causing Ophelia to lose major balance.

Tumbled on the ground, Zyra hesitates to reach out her hand to help Ophelia get up. Before she takes action, Ophelia gently smiles at her, "Don't worry, dear..." the prophet speaks as she elegantly sits up. The pain of her shattered claws causes her to wince up. Even with her eyes semi-closed, she remains enlightened with Zyra's attempt to reach over her.

"Before you go, let me thank you for your time by telling you where you will encounter the monster." Ophelia states. "That means that this prediction exclusively works for you, gatekeeper." Ophelia adds with a wink. Blank scoffs as he trudges away from the two. Noticing Blank's constant stomping, Zyra tilts her head. "You... You know where the monster is heading?" she questions curiously. "No, dear. *You* do." Ophelia smiles.

Blank didn't understand this odd comment from the zombified prophet. "Zoriadia..." he begins to ask with his voice slowly raising. "Is that monster someone you happen to *know?*" Blank gathers. "Of course! She knows our target better than anyone else! After all, they were both gatekeepers before the hatchening!" Ophelia chuckles before Zyra could have a chance to defend herself.

"I-I'm not a gatekeeper...! I mean, not anymore..." Zyra stutters. Blank observes the screaming denial in Zyra's eyes. The corruptive attitude of the masked leader grows over Zyra's stature – "Did you intentionally miss our target to let him free?" Blank grits. Zyra backs down upon hearing the question.

Blank nods to himself as if he understood Zyra's gestures. "H-Hold on! Let me explain! That monster, he's not, y'know, the same person I once knew!" Zyra hesitates to speak. "He even tried to unscarf me! I can't call him a... I can't call that *thing* a f-friend..." Zyra slows her words as she begins to sink her head. "So, don't get the wrong idea!" she nervously declares as Blank continues to nod to himself.

"It's okay! Now you know that the monster is really not as beautiful as we all thought!" Ophelia blurts. "Now, if you honestly remember Imporia like the back of your hand, you will encounter our target where he usually seeks peace." the prophet hints after her crown subtly ticks. Blank exhales, "What's the catch this time?" – "Resist my words and you shall perish too, Blank." the prophet playfully shoots back.

With a small hand of options, the masked man shelters his insecurities behind his unsteady frown. "Zoriadia... You know what happens to traitors." Blank intimidatingly states as he continues to tower over Zyra's fragile seriousness. "However, even if I wanted to erase you, this mission just became impossible without you." Blank scowls.

"Before we find this 'happy' place, let's gather the others." Blank states as he coldly begins to walk away.

With full force, Blank uses his sharp pin-arms to chop trees. With his path being cleared, Zyra ponders a bit before tagging along. "Gatekeeper, before you go..." Ophelia speaks before their reunion ends.

Perhaps I may have chosen the wrong gatekeeper to place my faith as a champion...

I didn't expect for our brilliant friend to get infected by that annoying parasite.

 *"Zyra"* downloaded. Category: Enemy.

Our monster is too hard to handle because of that robot... I've never seen anything like it.

Perhaps if we dispatch it, we can take multiple flaps of the champion's scarf and some of us can enjoy another chance at happiness!

Are you saying there's still a way to save him?

It's why Blanky-poo is dying to keep you under his belt — you're the only one that can stop it.

I'm counting on you to help me save Astra! If you do that, you can save all of the survivors left!

Ophelia declares her message. "Now, don't waste time! We all have a deadline coming up." she playfully adds after wiping her slightly dirty dress. Swallowing this pill of revelations burdens Zyra with a boulder on her back. She progressively turns her back at the prophet and begins to march her way towards Blank's direction. "...I'm not done with you, Thevenin." Zyra whispers to herself.

Chapter X:
Crashing Rampage

What does your heart earnestly beat for?

"...I'm retiring." Reza announces in monotone. The traumatic experience that Reza went through forces her to stay away from all types of combat. Pretty understandable for Grant after seeing Reza's eyes carry large dark baggage. While there was no reason to dismiss her into the void, the elder proposes the idea of letting Reza help develop a method to unify the scarfs they had previously collected. At least she may juice her tired efforts into discovering the exit the fort had dreamed of.

Obviously, risking her safety in the void wasn't worth leaving the fort. Consequently, she submissively follows the elder's recommendations. It was unusual for the hardheaded guardian to agree with ease, yet Grant resents sending her off into a treacherous mission without prior experience to defend herself.

Amphy perches his head onto her lap and silently embraces her as she returns a tight hug. "Amphy..." the depressed Reza speaks up with a small grin.

It was only moments later where Reza gets placed in the center of the damaged fort. The fort resembled a stone igloo – the structure of the building rises skywards, but the destroyed rooftops were concaved. The blinding white light of the colorless skies provided illumination for the dreary space. In the middle of the broken watchtower resided two men who fashioned green scarfs.

While these men had faces, Reza couldn't focus on their exact appearance. Each member wore similar attire to what the guardian had when exploring Void-Imporia; dark blue skin-tight undershirts and a chest pad. They weren't armed with shoulder pads or fancy weapons, instead, they had been tediously operating on the collection of cloth with metallic bars. The rushing collaborators hastily welcome Reza and hurriedly ask for her assistance.

With a fuzzy mentality, Reza follows the instructions of the men. It appears that they have been trying to mesh the colors of the scarf with various methods. Burnt scarves, rippled cloths, and wools with nails decorated the hollow watchtower. Reza quickly gets lost in exactly what she had to do. She only knew that she felt overwhelmed by creating a method to merge scarves together.

It all just blended and became one blurry experience for the deeply disturbed Reza. After harnessing a near-death experience and activating unmentioned trauma, she begins to act as if she were in autopilot. Everything regarding her will simply phases out of her mind.

Amphy patiently sits near the group of experimenters. At the edge of his vision, the youngster sees Grant leaving the fort. Stealthily, the curious boy makes his way to the elder and asks where he was going. "My boy, even if Reza manages to find a way to combine all of the scarves, we're still short of colors." the elder gently explains.

Watching the elder leave the fort to scur his unknown plans, Amphy simply watches. In the horizon of his sight, he sees another, distant figure. The young boy winces his eyes to see his dolls being held by a hooded figure. Impulsively, the child jumps to himself and runs off to reclaim his adored doll, Mister Poo.

. . .

Anxious from her silent walk with the anger-pointed Blank, the two eventually reach the entrance of the arena. The remaining red-scarfed Aphotic members halt their movement. Blank particularly stops Zyra from getting inside the arena. "Zoriadia..." the masked man pauses, alerting Zyra.

"There's a big burden placed on your shoulders." Blank speaks up as Zyra patiently listens. "I can understand that this void is troubling you and such, but Aphotic is counting on you. And I know – you didn't ask for this. I know I forced you to join our legion unlike many others. But that being said..." Blank declares.

Hearing his transparency alarmed Zyra. She gives him a definite glance, but guises a worried expression. Blank, understanding her? Zyra couldn't fathom his previous statement, yet anxiously listens to what he has to say next.

I haven't had the time to pause and...

Well, um, thank you for your service.

...Why grateful all of a sudden?

I'd easily tell you to stop wasting my breathe, yet if it weren't for you, I would've lost the election out of impulse.

...You're weird. I'm not your therapist, okay?

Next time I get too impulsive, I want you to be the one to calm me down, Zoriadia. Can you do me that favor?

...You expect too much from strangers, y'know?

Don't be fooled by kindness, gatekeeper.

Hearing his words followed by a large smirk threatens Zyra. Momentarily, Blank finally enters the arena to catch hordes of Aphotic members vigorously discussing results of their exploration through the void. "Mister Blank! Finally, you're back!" shouts one masked member from a distance.

"We've scavenged all over the void only to find boring colors!" — "No signs of any new colors!" — "Where were you just now?" — "What happened to the blue team?" A plethora of questions crashes onto the boggle-minded leader.

Moments later, Blank stands in the center of the arena confidently and addresses his legion about certain issues. In his bickering, the masked leader demands the group to divide themselves and orders them to search for a humanoid monster that wears a lavish magenta scarf. In his loud speech, he calls out for Zyra.

"Zoriadia! According to that damned prophet, you should know where our target should reside." Blank leans over to give Zyra the spotlight.

With practically an array of Aphotic members awaiting her command, she takes a couple of seconds to gather what this 'peaceful' place could have been.

Blank's silent gleam initially fills Zyra with dread. This entire opportunity blindly glows in her hands. How shall she carry out her revenge? "Um…" Zyra ponders timidly. Seeing the legion of Aphotic surrounding her again built up a roaring anxiety. Oddly enough, with a lack of blue-scarfs in the fleet, all of the faceless minions surged Zyra with a sudden feeling of power.

Leadership was never her forte – Zyra easily shies away from large crowds. However, with this many vicious hunters ready to follow any order, Zyra's plan at revenge was just fingertips away.

"Ahem, um…" Zyra hesitates weakly. She glances at Viola from a distance and remembers noting her two scarfs. Additionally, seeing that the legion was composed of only green and yellow scarfs continues to shove a message in her face. "So… Of the time I knew that, um, monster, there were *two* places he'd always be at no matter what…" Zyra sheepishly announces.

"Two? Well, we can divide teams if we need to assure our success." Blank heartily suggests. "They are…" Zyra mumbles. She begins to mouth the instructions to the pending legion as the team rallies up.

. . .

Ultimately, Aphotic members carry out their leader's orders while Zyra decides to stay back. Watching events ensue in front of her, she ponders about her choices. Scratched up and in doubt, the cold-hearted gatekeeper hears Viola gently approaching her.

The entire arena empties out its inhabitants, leaving only the gatekeeper and the masked maiden to guard the arena until all members returned. Viola continues to scoot near Zyra and begins to poke into her personal space. "You're very nice to stay and guard me!" Viola cheerfully expresses. Zyra then pulls out her blade and aims it at Viola's neck. "Zoriadia?" the masked lady calmly calls out the gatekeeper's nickname. "Everyone wearing a mask is as blind as they come…" Zyra snickers.

"...Did I do something wrong, Zoriadia?" Viola questions. "No one is here to protect you. Now, I want answers. You are going to give it to me. Otherwise, you'll be joining the rest of the island, understood?" Zyra coldly prompts. "Oh? I'd love to chat!" the masked maiden calmly states.

The masked maiden couldn't pertain herself. She gets giddy to the point where she places her puppet hands over Zyra's blade and tucks it away. "Oh! Didn't you see the *Void Master* yet!?" Viola jumpily states. Zyra spirals in awe as Viola completely deflects her blade without any issues.

"See, I've been theorizing that in this entire void, the champion to-be has a massive advantage from all of the other competitors because they must be directly associating with a void master!" Viola speeches as Zyra continues to stare at her blade in disbelief. "What does that mean?" the baffled gatekeeper asks.

"I was trying to voice my theory to Blank earlier because I am absolutely certain that the void master is no other than the talking egg on the monster's back." Viola declares. "...Talking egg? ...Are you talking about, uh, the robot? Sympl?" Zyra reports.

"Is that what it's called? A void master takes many forms and shapes. Normally, they are talking colorless objects that give their host an unspeakable ability..." Viola states. Zyra continues to ponder upon her recent encounter and focuses on Sympl's behavior.

"Okay, big deal. What's the problem with letting anyone win in the first place then, huh? Are you afraid of making people happy? Is that why you're working to make everyone miserable?" Zyra chatters. Viola negatively nods, "Zoriadia, winning an election implies the complete destruction of the void. Anyone left behind will perish regardless of who they are." Viola morbidly states.

"Winning the election eliminates everyone from the void?" Zyra harshly questions in despair. Viola nods her head calmly as Zyra releases a heavy sigh. "If you want to stop the election to save survivors, then why the heck are you all so keen on destroying innocent people!?" the gatekeeper blurts with violence.

"I do not know how to word this correctly, but destruction births creation. If all survivors fall, including the upcoming champion, then the election cannot be complete and perhaps then we may have a *null-exit point*." Viola speeches. "What the hell does that even mean?" Zyra confusingly screeches.

"Frankly, I do not expect you to understand. Blank and I have a very detailed plan on how we are going about the election. The most important thing is to secure and prevent the spread of the champion's scarf, eliminate all survivors and imprison all void masters." Viola explains as her words continue to baffle the analytical Zyra.

"You're insane... You plan on murdering those in Aphotic as well, aren't you?" Zyra's heaping angry rises. "That is not necessarily in the current plan, at least Blank doesn't want any more accidents from now on. In fact, he promised to protect those in his team which is why you should heavily consider staying loyal to him." Viola genuinely speeches. "You don't believe that, do you? Blank can't even keep a straight face!" – "I do and I've pledged myself to helping him." Viola coldly replies.

"Blank didn't even shed a tear when Headless got torn to shreds! You call that empathy!?" Zyra spouts out. "To be fair, Headless was perfect for being Blank's shield..." Viola eerily comments without any regard for the fallen companion. "You're sick..." Zyra replies. "You don't care about life either, do you?" – "Again, destructions births creation." Viola responds.

Zyra begins to break a sweat and even cycles in circles. "Fine... You two want to destroy everything before the election does. Then why not help Ophelia and her loophole idea instead?" – "What's that?" – "She wants to win the election to stop the Astra from dying or something. Doesn't that mean she could, in theory, stop time and let us all live forever?" Zyra questions to the talkative Viola.

"Zoriadia, you've been mistaken! We currently *are* in the after-life and we currently *are* living forever. Even with these conditions, you can't escape death — just look at your scarf. It's been damaged and that's enough to endanger you out of this eternity. Using another chance at happiness to lock yourself into this void... It's illogical and just not safe! If your mortality depends on the scarf you wear, how can we ensure that it'll stay on you forever? It's simply better if we evaded this void, break the system, and force another way out!" Viola explains.

"W-Well...!" Zyra has a loss of words with Viola's compelling argument. "Then why can't we all just stop this useless slashing and get along or something?" Zyra mumbles as Viola gently glints at her. "Do you pretend that survivors like yourself have the decency to appreciate this unworldly emptiness? You're imperfect, Zyra. You cannot attempt to make a system of peace when you yourself already invalidated it." Viola coldly states.

Zyra, ready to bark back at Viola for her daring assumptions glances at Viola's twin-tied neck. The dangling green scarf on her neck flaps in innocence. The gatekeeper stares at the fallen scarf and is reminded of her tainted actions. Quick flashbacks of all the wrong her had done rushes through her head and is humbled by Viola's honesty.

"Regardless, it's useless to 'team-up' with non-Aphotic members when void masters are roaming freely. They are the root of the scarf's expiration, y'know?" Viola states coldly. "Also, next time you point your blade at me, please remember that I'm only here to stop void masters, not what you call 'innocents' or however you perceive these problematic obstacles."

Completely baffled by the animated puppet, Zyra struggles to understand Aphotic's intentions. Having Viola spelling it out in obvious ways refreshed Zyra's circumstances, yet her logic was mysterious and even morbid to the gatekeeper. Aggravated by the thought of how Aphotic continuously discards life as if it were nothing boiled the gatekeeper's blood. With a hesitation on words to say, Zyra asks her final question.

"Answer me this then. Why are you more concerned about void masters than Imporians? Isn't that little robot just that? A little robot?" Zyra asks. Upon saying it aloud, she begins to ponder on why Ophelia continued to pester the gatekeeper about the robot. What did she mean by parasite? Why is Viola so critical on ridding the accused Sympl?

"As you expected, a void master doesn't rely on a scarf to survive." Viola's words directed. "They aren't eligible to win an election. That's why they force their host to win. If they do win..." Viola anxiously states.

"Truthfully, I'm unsure and I do not want to explore that possibility either! Point is, if a void master is the last thing alive, without its host, all of us will forever be imprisoned as piles of ash for the rest of time." Viola cheerfully states as Zyra finds her words jarring. "Think about it like eternal gatekeepers that prevent souls from moving on." Viola sinisterly adds.

"Hah! But it's all okay! We don't have to worry about that! Aphotic won't ever let that happen! In a few moments, Blank and his army will retrieve the scarf you sent them to, right?" Viola jollily asks. Zyra's silent expression coupled with a small drip of sweat grows onto Viola. "You *did* send Aphotic to hunt down the monster, right...?"

The gatekeeper nervously stares at the masked maiden in silence.

. . .

Time passes by.

The masked leader finds himself on the outskirts of the island. His shoes softly dig into colorless dunes. Mellowed, he begins to analyze the still ocean. The static waves fail to produce any movement and eerily blend with the sky. "Place of peace, huh?" he mutters to himself, pondering about the target's passion for silent shores.

Lost in thought, one of his comrades breaks his daze, "Mister Blank, there are some very faint but large footprints over here!" With a disrupted daze, Blank readily prepares to request the team to follow the trail when another comrade spouts, "Actually, I think that was me! Sorry."

The leader bites himself and rapidly taps his foot. For what had felt like an endless search, he finds himself growing uneasy by the second. "That prophet and her lies..." Blank sighs dreadfully. Scattering sands from the distance faintly grew louder. The leader's racing thoughts halt upon realizing that something was approaching the group. Disturbed by the sound of plowing sand, Blank transforms his red arms into their signature pin form.

A small stranger arises from one of the mountainous dune's horizons. As a reaction, dozens of Aphotic members quickly drew their weapons. "Ready, Aphotic!" Blank announces. The approaching figure slowly reaches the top of the towering dune. The figure rubs its eyes in order to focus on what was possibly making the mummering. Blank hesitates on calling out a command – it wasn't the fabled target but a young, frightened boy.

"Hold fire." Blank announces, making all members ease up in unison. Amphy slips over the pile of sand, shortly rolling towards the crowd. Once he gets up and sporadically pats himself, he learns that Aphotic had been observing the clumsy boy's movements from a safe distance. "H-Hunters!" Amphy screams to himself.

Blank signals another gesture to keep his legion at ease. The leader then approaches the young boy who had been too shocked to make a run for it. It only took a couple of steps for Blank to reach the terrified youngster. The leader then sees his yellow scarf, bushy hair and freezes once he gets a glance at the boy's childlike facial structure.

Debating on whether the color would be useful or not, Blank tactically observes the fear-induced boy. Scanning the entire area to see that his teammates were also wearing a mix of yellow and green scarves, the leader coldly concludes what should be done.

Amphy pants loudly due to fear, yet Blank takes a quiet approach. The masked man bends over to the lost child and reverts his pins back to his red arms. "This isn't a safe place to wander around, child." Blank states. Amphy immediately recollects himself and scatters his footing to stand up.

In the span of seconds, Grant makes an appearance over the greatly elevated dune that the youngster had tripped from. The elder sees the row of Aphotic members and spots Amphy's jumpiness. Momentarily, the members shift their attention to the elder who held a cane like a rifle. Aphotic drew their weapons once again, eager to defend their leader from the unexpected elder's appearance.

"Hunters!" Grant calls out. Blank moves his head upwards seeing the elder tower above him. Before Blank could react to anything, he starts to get up only to hear Grant unnervingly say, "You'll pay for all the lives you took!" Without much time to react, Blank then hears the elder's cane cocking followed by a piercing gunshot.

Distantly floating above everyone's heads, the Astra's green ribbon suddenly wraps itself up, declaring its expiration. With the loss of the free-flowing appendage, a bell rings across the entirety of the void. Once the bell could be heard, a minor shockwave vibrates throughout the blank island. This creates deeper scratch marks and now, raw patches of grass. These green leaves were far and few, unlike the metallic bars that continued to erect higher into the skies and the icy crystal shards that grew sharper.

Those who had an emerald green cloth woven on their necks were missing in action. The vibration gradually comes to a quiet end and reminds the survivors about the remaining ribbons left. With three appendages now folded into petal-like shapes, the Astra nears to its final ribbons.

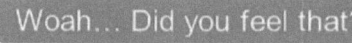 Woah... Did you feel that?

Yes, another vibration. This is the second time I've recorded such a quake.

Second time? This has to be the fourth time it's rung or something!

Volt, it appears that you're sweating. Are you feeling okay?

 I-I'm fine...

He then glances at his trembling palms. Feeling the shockwave reminded him of his heroic attempt at saving the citizens at the collapsing city. He couldn't handle the fact that he doesn't know the fate of the roaming Imporians. "I-I'm not sweating." he denies as his mind races upon the endless questions he generates. He clears his dry throat and silently mutters to himself, "Where now...?"

"Instead of seeking shelter, why don't we find a place that brings you peace of mind?" Sympl suggests. Surprised, Volt shifts into remaining silent upon hearing his partner's suggestion. "Besides, judging from your paralyzing heart-rate, it seems that you may need a vacation." Sympl adds on. "Stop doing that." – "Doing what?" – "Analyzing me." The duo converse with Volt's uncomfortable tone shutting down Sympl.

"...Analytics strongly suggest that you will overheat if you continue to—" – "Sympl, shut up!" Volt tackles back upon hearing the robotic backpack's persistent buzzing. This makes Sympl emit a sad-beep. "Oh, you think you can guilt me now?" Volt queries.

In a turn of events, Sympl does what was requested which results in Volt receiving the silent treatment. The sweating monster continues to aimlessly walk throughout the void. Resenting his sudden aggression on the only one that literally had his back, he begins to fathom where he was located in the void. With the raw patches of grass spouting in the colorless environment, Volt slowly is reminded of a colorful garden he'd pour his free time in.

Chapter XI:
Treacherous Libertatum

How long will you endure before you give up?

Broken from her purposeless gaze, Reza screams in utter horror as she witnesses fort members with green scarfs violently evaporating into thin hot air. The pained screeching of her associates fades into the void's empty skies, traumatizing her reality. Petrified, she drops to the ground and defensively curls up.

With what little energy the evaporating bodies had left, the steaming figures desperately reach out towards Reza's neck. They eventually grope onto her body, causing Reza to absolutely blow up. She heartlessly pushes the decapitating bodies away from her, "Let go of me!" She tears up. Even with an undying will, these victims fail to yank her scarf in timely fashion. The last-second betrayal her associates demonstrated had shaken Reza's core.

Once all bodies vanished without a single trace, nausea strikes her. The world, despite it being completely empty, spun on her head and she was tempted to relieve herself. Reza struggles to get up as her dizzy state shackled her current position. In full force, she attempts to vomit, yet absolutely nothing comes out.

Heavily sickened by the immaculate fear and unexplainable evaporation, she scowls for air. The heat that condenses in the room where she had been desperately attempting to understand the rainbow theory fogs her. Reza ultimately crawls out of the enclosed room and quickly realizes that the fort was completely empty.

All members were gone – only their glowing green scarves were left on the void's floors. Sweating from the heat and feeling faint, Reza screams, "Amphy!" followed by a gag. She could not find the only reason why she deals with the fort – Amphy had gone missing. Reza screams and shouts the young boy's name again, yet no response at all.

Her roars become heartbroken cries as tears rush out of her distorted eyes. Out of dire desperation, Reza cries out the name of Grant. She had never placed all of her hope in this last resort – yet Grant does not respond for he too is missing.

Reza cries for someone, something – anything to help her locate Amphy. As she screams with her head pointed skyward, she notices that the eerie cloth-covered star continues to statically float. Half of itself had appendages while the other half composed of petal-like shapes. With her insanity spreading like wildfire, she grabs her hefty paintbrush from where she left it and impulsively runs. She runs along the direction of the yellow appendage in her last attempt to search for Amphy.

. . .

Blank gargles in unstoppable pain for as a searing bullet had just pierced his shoulder. The masked man falls to his knees, dripping an uncomfortable amount of blood. Grant licks his lips and unlocks his sight of his cane-rifle. He turns around to quickly see how remaining Aphotic members charge at him. Half of the squad were in the mist of evaporating into nothingness as their emerald green scarves no longer were effective in the void.

Those that wore yellow rallied up towards Grant without question. With Aphotic's array of sharp melee weapons charging towards the elder, Grant yells, "Cover your ears, Amphy!" The inanimate boy, already deafened from the first loud blow, refuses to move a muscle after seeing how Grant blew Blank's shoulder off.

Grant rampages his rifle as he sprays bullets through the sandy shores. Aphotic members that razzle in searing pain lifelessly drop their carcasses on the blank sands. Even after receiving such a fatal hit, some members continued to struggle on getting back on their feet.

After all members had swiftly been grounded, Grant cracks his knuckles and nods to himself. He then sluggishly jogs by and yank the scarves of every member who had their bleeding bodies on the ground. This entire sequence was rhythmic and fast-paced. Aphotic members who still had enough courage to grab the elder's leg were simply kicked over and relieved of their scarves.

Having absolutely no context of the situation, Amphy uses this opportunity to climb the same dune he had come from. Little footprints he had left behind eventually blended itself into back into the empty void. Regardless, Amphy tries his best to backtrack and runs in fear of his life.

With just a handful of Aphotic members left to unscarf, Grant finally approaches Blank.

Grant then glocks his cane.

You with all of your tally marks... Identify yourself.

Kah... You really know how to get a king's attention, huh?

So you are the leader of Aphotic as I assumed. Where's your shame?

Shame? Hah... I left it with your dentures, old man.

Very funny clown. Now perish.

H-Hey hold up! I'm goi—

Without further ado, Grant yanks Blank's scarf off. The masked man begins to freak out as he feels immense heat getting to him. Not only did the pain of being pierced prevent him from moving properly but the evaporation process begins to fry his functioning nerves.

"Heh, time to pay for your sins." Grant snorts. As Blank began to glow, Grant suddenly breaks a sweat. The elder begins to heavily breathe and then eventually glows as well. "What in tarnation..." he questions with a bit of concern in his tone. Here, Blank cracks one of the widest smirks he has ever produced.

"Boy, do I got have some news for you!" Blank snickers. "The hell did you do to me...?" Grant points back, whiffing his shirt. With the remaining adrenaline in his body, Blank extends one of his pin arms to its maximum length in order to reclaim his fallen scarf. He successfully nabs his red scarf from Grant's grip and rapidly adjusts it over his neck once again. This halts the entire evaporation process as a whole.

Now without anyway to move, Grant grunts. Impressed with Blank's transformable pin-arms, Grant attempts to snag the scarf one more time.

However, upon swiping his hand, he completely misses because he lacks a hand. Grant then realizes his entire arm is fading out of existence. The elder begins to scream in agony. "It's been an honor for you to be my next tally-mark, pal." Blank proudly says as Grant continues to dissipate.

"But... How come!? I'm wearing my scarf..." Grant regretfully speaks in a pinch. The elder yet again attempts to steal Blank's scarf with his other hand only to make the same conclusion – he lacks arms. "How come...!" Grant struggles to pronounce as his voice grew sloppier by the moment.

"How come..." Grant says as he comes to terms. All of the elder's atoms had dissipated into hot air and were collected into the vast void of Imporia.

Blank drops the heaviest exhale. He lays completely flat on the soothing sands and soaks in the heat of the moment. On the verge of possibly fainting, the remaining Aphotic members struggle to approach him with their wounds. Precisely three of the dozen Aphotic members had survived Grant's rampage. He rolls his head at the remaining henchmen.

"I think it's time we used the big guns." Blank announces. And, well, momentarily, the leader had shamefully returned to the arena once again. Viola and Zyra were not only surprised, but in shock of Blank's malformed state. He then hastily explains the recent events.

"So, you're telling me there was a guy with a gun and that's why you don't have a working shoulder anymore?" Zyra dastardly questions upon greeting the injured Blank with his few remaining henchmen.

"Yeah, he's gone. N-No big deal, heh. I just, uh, need you to continue the hunt. If the m-monster sees me in these conditions, he might just have an advantage over me..." Blank sheepishly requests. Zyra and Viola give each other an odd look. "Blank, how about you send me out instead?" Viola curiously asks. Zyra clears her throat, "Fear not, Viola. This is a perfect opportunity for me to finish the job." Zyra confidently states.

Without hesitating, Zyra amasses the remaining yellow Aphotic members and leads them out of the arena. Zyra silently snickers to herself as she had just successfully escaped Blank's clingy palms with a portion of his legion under her belt.

Chapter XII:
United by Oath

To sustain is to pay for life...

"Amphy!" Reza cries out in despair. In the nearby horizons, she encounters an approaching, short-statured figure. Shaken, Reza calls out the name once more with no results of a response. She doesn't hesitate to madly dash towards the youngster.

Before reaching Amphy, she drops her metallic paintbrush, lifts the young figure, and spins him with joy. Except, the boy was startled and reacted with screaming. Quickly, Amphy realizes that he was properly abducted by Reza. "R-Reza!" Amphy blurts.

Her tears of stress burst into joy as she had been reunited with her reason of defense. Her face was of happiness and relief.

She takes a moment to gracefully stare into Amphy's eyes. Inaudibly, the young boy could not hear anything she mouthed. His focus on Reza's distorted face in combination with his listening issues causes him to notice how much dread was written across her face.

"Reza, I can't hear you..." Amphy directly says, converting Reza's graceful wincing into one of disturbance. No matter what Reza was trying to say, it simply wasn't understood. She continues to speak to no avail. Amphy tilts his head in frustration when suddenly Reza lifts her index finger.

She winces her eyebrows in defeat, but remained exuberant over their reunion. Reza takes a moment to pick up and flip her paintbrush, placing the brush side of it the floor. Amphy patiently waits for what Reza had been attempting to communicate until sudden horror hits him.

With the sharpest part of her paintbrush facing upwards, Reza slowly takes in a deep breath and slits her arm. Evidently, Amphy exclaims revulsion as he demands for Reza to stop her act of self-harm. However, upon seeing her drenching red arm, Reza slowly approaches the alarmed boy and wipes her blood over his golden scarf.

Resistive, Amphy yet again tells Reza to stop her disgusting act. With the yellow scarf being painted a bloody red, Reza grows fainter by the moment. Even if the petrified youngster fails to hear anything, Reza speaks to herself. "Promises aren't meant to be broken, Amphy..."

As her red blood soaks and overwrites the golden yellow colors on the boy's scarf, a faint humming is heard. Relieved that Amphy had his color promoted, Reza gently smiles. "How does it feel... to cheat death..." Reza slurs.

Her ill body crashes onto the floor. Immediately, Amphy cries out. "Reza! Reza!" Even when grounded, she barely continues to leave her tear eyes open. "It's okay, Amphy... You're going to be safe and that's all that matters." Reza murmurs weakly.

"Well that's just no good!" Ophelia interrupts. In their environment, the two siblings note the distant figure approaching them. At first, Reza firmly believes she was just staring at a hallucination, yet the eager prophet budges her way into their sight. "And to think we still have some competitors after all." Ophelia adds as she directs her attention to the floored lady, who continues to leak bodily fluids.

Her mysterious presence felt unwelcomed and insidious. Yet, the sibling's direct situation granted them a moment of respite. The lack of Ophelia wearing a mask gave them hopes that she was not an acclaimed hunter or a source of violence.

Ophelia doesn't hesitate on pulling out leftover cloth from her sachet. She extracts her stitching toolkit and the stolen Mr. Poo doll Amphy had previously possessed. Amphy's eyes blare open when he sees the prophet pull out his wooled possession. "This is going to hurt a bit, but will stop your pouring." Ophelia announced.

. . .

Prosperous with colors this time, Volt had arrived at a dismantled garden. No trees, no buildings, no signs of life. Only the duo, bright green grass and a plethora of flowers all in an everlastingly wide plain.

"Systems have regulated for optimal performance." Sympl beeps out. The robotic backpack and the forsaken Imporian aimlessly roam the empty island. "Now since we're at our destination, perhaps you should practice socializing more often. It would be useful to your health."

"Or maybe just take a moment to be one with the flowers." Volt exhales. "The flower bed may be appealing, but should this be your priority?" Sympl replies. "Mind your business, Sympl." Volt shoots back.

 Is there an issue, Master Volt?

Admit it. There's no point in going on.

 Morbid thought process? That is very unlike you, Volt. We must continue to—

Continue to what? Keep roaming endlessly? There's literally nothing to do.

 Boredom? If you so desire so, I could reprogram myself into a video game for you to play with.

I've had enough of these games. Now you're just making excuses to stay on my back, Sympl.

 Volt, I am here to protect ourselves at all costs. It is vital that you understand this.

You're only saying that because you want me for my body, not because of some program.

 Negative. This unit will ensure your safety in exchange for the voltage you are storing.

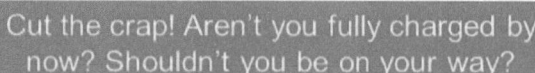 Cut the crap! Aren't you fully charged by now? Shouldn't you be on your way?

 Sympl is unable to predict such an outcome where separation would benefit us.

The tiny robot continues to eagerly beep and argues against the Imporian's deluded thinking. The flustered Volt then tries to remove the

120

robotic backpack. He grabs Sympl and forcefully nudges the companion out of his back, only for the robot to tighten its grip around Volt's chest.

"Volt! I will not allow you to make rash decisions!" Sympl blurts outwards. Volt struggles on pushing his companion away, only to run out of breath from the cable's contractions. He takes a heavy breath and then attempts to push Sympl again. This time, the robot lightly zaps Volt to stop him.

Shocked by the robot, Volt groans in pain. "Sympl!" he mutters belligerently. "This unit will not release Volt... Not yet." Sympl states back flaring red light from its lens. The Imporian begins to pant heavily and even breaks a sweat. Hearing his companion raise its own robotic tone to place a demand got Volt nervous. "Why are you so persistent?" the Imporian asks in disbelief.

Struggling to get his backpack out of him, Volt draws a cold conclusion. "No, don't tell me..." Volt growls. "You won't let me go because *you* want to win the damn election, huh?" Volt interrogates. Followed by his questioning, the robot instantly beeps, "Error detected!" The Imporian struggles to strangle his companion, "Answer me, dammit!" he mutters.

Once the alarm went off, Volt turns back to unsurprisingly be greeted by Zyra. This time, she was with a group of Aphotic members. Without hesitation, Sympl raises its tactical wires.

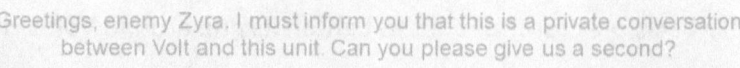
Greetings, enemy Zyra. I must inform you that this is a private conversation between Volt and this unit. Can you please give us a second?

And I thought you wanted to party.

Zyra...

Due to how the duo and Aphotic stood in the endless gardens, Sympl announces, "Warning! Surrounded battle inbound. Unable to route an escape route." Upon hearing this, Volt understands that hiding is virtually impossible given that there were no tangible structures to seek shelter.

"You shall not touch Volt." Sympl defensively announces aloud. "Too bad. I'm not taking orders anymore." Zyra snappily replies. She tauntingly looks at her blade then locks her eyes at her target. "Sympl, dammit! Let go of me already!" Volt stammers. "This unit refuses to go down without you, Volt." Sympl eerily declares.

Lacking patience, the Aphotic members charge at Volt with their various weapons in their hands. Initiating the ambush, Sympl wraps its tactical cable arms around the scarf's loose appendages. One of the cables darts itself at the floor and forces Volt to take a side-step, dodging one of the member's sharp strikes.

"I'm not your puppet, Sympl!" Volt roars, ready to take over the driver's seat. "You are my host and I shall follow your instructions! However, that also implies that this entire unit should not be damaged either." Sympl beeps.

Momentarily, another devious ambusher springs into the air and aims their blade at Volt. The Imporian reaches out his hand, indicating Sympl to grab the airborne opponent. Without realizing it, the airborne Aphotic member gets tangled up by two of Sympl's cables.

Another Aphotic ally tries to free their wrapped comrade by readying their knife. Volt's grab gesture swings into a palm gesture, commanding Sympl to slap the ally with the entangled member. In the meantime, another foe directly targets Volt. The Imporian then holds out finger-guns.

Once again, Sympl reads his partner's hand signal and sprays a small dose of incubated electricity at the offender. With the burning sparks trickling around the target's body, Sympl then strikes the member away by thrusting more of its cords against its chest.

All of these simultaneous actions began to overwhelm Aphotic. Each member gives each other a distinct stare and a silent nod. In the span of just a few seconds, all members began to relentlessly charge at the Imporian at the same time. Volt strikes his hand at the skies and twirls his index finger. All of Sympl's cables began to rotate like a copter which violently spins himself and his backpacking partner.

The Imporian hurdles like a hurricane, aggressively slapping all of the nearby Aphotic members and ultimately blows them away with a powerful gust of wind. Volt fabulously ends his dance then points at Zyra. He then curls his finger at her, making Sympl's cable mimic the same gesture. Taunted, the gatekeeper finally takes her stance. Zyra refuses to hold back and sprints at the synchronized duo.

As the two were holding off against each other, Volt roars.

Cutting my leg and joining those damn hunters... You're a failure of a gatekeeper!

At first, I was protecting what was important to *me*...

What the hell was more important than saving the Imporians when they needed us!?

It was you, Thevenin! You were more important than those islanders!

H-Huh!? L-Liar!

What have you become...? You truly cannot be Thevenin if you forgot about our time together...

...

Looks like you're right — Thevenin died a long time ago... And that's *your* fault. You're going to pay for all the harm you've done!

Hearing her genuine words pierced through Volt, which causes him to falter his stance for a mere second. The gatekeeper takes advantage of this by pushing Volt away with her sword. Sympl reacts to this by covering Volt from the lashing area, resulting in the loss of a cable arm.

Sympl screeches, "Error! Arm slot number four disengaged! Drawing more void energy to stabilize tactical operations." Without warning, the robot begins to drain electricity from Volt's body, shocking him in the process. The Imporian weakly grunts the robot's name in anger. Due to the sheer pain Volt had been inflicted upon, he finds himself temporarily paralyzed.

With the target completely immobile, all members of Aphotic quickly grab their dropped weapons and frantically rush to get up. Zyra then distantly points at the fallen target with her blade, conducting the group of Aphotic to eliminate Volt.

Chapter XIII:
A World Ending Chime

How much time do you really have left?

In the colorless skies, the Astra's yellow ribbon finally expires. With its golden ribbon coiling up, the sound of a loud bell starts to chime across the entire plain of Void Imporia. As the explosive shockwave scatters throughout the empty island, cracks extend and tectonic shards spike out of the blank grounds. Grass grew mossy, crystal shards were sharper and metallic bars rose even higher. With the inclusion of these rippling tectonic plates, soft carroty dirt could be found in between large cracks of the floor.

. . .

Aphotic members initiate deadly strikes to take the Imporian's velvet scarf. During their attack, they were interrupted by an unexplainable shock of heat. These members drop everything and begin to screech in pain. The intense heat came from none other than the melting vibration that roared across the entire void. In efforts to relieve themselves of the scorching pain, some members forfeited their scarfs and ceased to exist. Determined members attempt to bash through the pain and continue to fight the immobile Imporian. However, their physical bodies would only remain intact for a couple of moments before evaporating into nothingness.

The stern expression Volt carried hindered into one of relief. Yet, witnessing a mass of people evaporate horrendously in front of his very eyes quickly fills him with sorrow. Speechless, Volt struggles to stand on his two feet. "What... What just happened?" the confused Imporian questions.

He was too psyched-out to comprehend the fact that his enemies just melted in thin air.

In dismay, Zyra lowers her sword. Left stranded with the Imporian and his hot robotic backpack, the gatekeeper releases a stressful scream. "You could've prevented that, you freak." Zyra begins to have one of her episodic panic attacks. Volt's face softens in disbelieve. He pokes up his posture to regain his strength, "What do you mean I could've prevented this!?" he shouts.

Zyra decides to slowly approach the weakened duo and stealthily draws her blade. "I'll make you regret pulling my scarf." Zyra then sprints at Volt, railing her blade on the ground. She springs up into the air and elegantly swipes her blade with all of her strength. Using the defensive tactical cables, Sympl counters the strike but breaks another armed wire. Zyra falls back and stays grounded due to electrical currents shocking her. The robotic backpack suffers another loss and demands to draw more power to stabilize its tactical state.

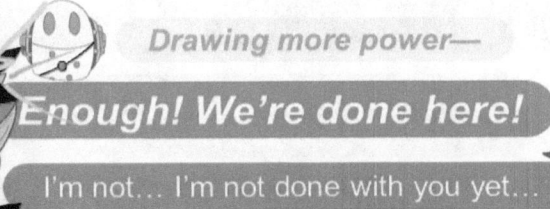

Tiny fumes and bright sparks emit from the damaged backpack. The gatekeeper remains locked onto the ground and the Imporian uses this moment to prepare his escape. Before he runs away however, he examines Zyra's numbness and sees spurs of bright sparks jolting around her armor. She groans in pain and ultimately fails to get up.

Seeing her in this weak state bothered Volt. He was ready to abandon her; a choice he wishes he could avoid. "I can't believe it's come to this..." Volt shrugs. The Imporian loathsomely exhales and turns his back at her, making Sympl face Zyra. "After all the crap I had to deal with... You're easily the biggest headache." Volt angrily says.

The struggling gatekeeper crawls at the Imporian and tries to catch his shin. Upon swiping her hand, she misses his leg. "Stop being so stubborn, Zyra." Volt dreadfully replies, almost stepping on her slim hands.

"If what you say about the Astra is true, that means by winning, I get some chance at happiness right? Isn't that what Ophelia said?" the Imporian asks himself wonderingly. His robotic companion beeps and replays a voice clip that he had recorded of Ophelia. "Replaying Ophelia's recorded dialogue..." Sympl announces as its tone begins to mimic that of the Impish lady.

Truthfully, I don't think you'll like to hear this, but the ribbons represent how much time is left.

No, silly! If *we* win the election, then I can solve the void's biggest issue!

Oops! Looks like I forgot to mention that part! Well, good job for doing your homework, Champion!

No, get this! If Champion saves the Astra, he can save me and countless of survivors!
*All you need to do is **hand me your scarf!***

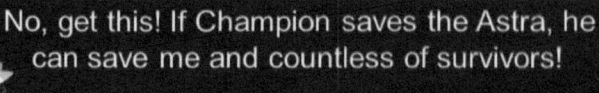

"Alright Sympl, shut it." Volt demands upon realizing that the robot did not automatically stop when necessary. Silent, the gatekeeper grew pale when she hears the robotic backpack recall bits of Ophelia's voice. The thought of the prophet gingerly treating Volt boils her blood. She recalls the prophet hinting Aphotic to get rid of a monster, yet hearing an alternate version of Ophelia felt bizarre.

"Wait! H-Hold up! So, how did the prophet lady know that the magenta scarf would 'win' from the start?" Volt sporadically questions, stopping any possible movement. He continues to ponder on the thought and starts drawing conclusions. "Perhaps it may be the work of—" Sympl suggests before Volt interrupts with, "Oh! She's a *prophet*, duh... how did that go over my head?" he answers himself and releases a sheepish laugh. Sympl remains quiet and slowly places the palm of its cable over its face.

The monstrous Imporian reveals one of the few joyful expressions that reminded Zyra of Thevenin's silly attitude. Volt's cheery face mildly turns into one of ease. "You've been talking to... You've been talking to Ophelia?" Zyra weakly pronounces, catching Volt's attention. "Couple of times. We're not friends or anything like that though." Volt bluntly replies.

"T-That doesn't make sense... The prophet never wanted you to win..." Zyra calls out. Volt relaxes his tense stance only to give the gatekeeper a spiteful look. "That's pretty obvious. We're already on bad terms." he sarcastically replies. "I don't think you understand... She never wanted *any* of us to win..." Zyra states.

"Isn't that obvious? 'Champion, Champion! We're going to win the election.' C'mon, at this rate, she's probably the same person that single-handedly triggered the hatchening in the first place." Volt childishly mocks Ophelia's soft voice. "Anyway, you won't stop me, Zyra." Volt harshly states.

Hearing all of his cold remarks in the flower-filled garden saddens the floored gatekeeper. "This isn't you T-Thevenin. You're a monster..." Zyra exhausts. "You promised me you'd never let any other survivors melt again..." the gatekeeper firmly declares. Of course, Volt takes these words lightly. "Pathetic! You still think I'm the problem here?" With a silent gap, he ponders on her determined expression for too long.

"Can't you remember?" Zyra hints. With the steam still wafting around the garden, small amounts of flower petals flutter around in the hot air. Volt's eyes sharpen once he grasps the pure familiarity of the garden he stands at. "This p-place, isn't where you find peace..." Zyra speaks up, still paralyzed from Sympl's jolting attack.

"This is where we met, remember?" Zyra precisely claims. Hearing her statement tears down his stern expression into one of holding back. This temporarily reverts Volt into his former, careless self.

. . .

Thevenin remembers how the entire garden was engulfed in flames. Horrendous voices screech for their lives, gatekeepers of all kinds rush around, and thick smoke circles the immediate area like an inferno. Just like how the injured Zyra helplessly lays on the ground, Volt is taken back to the time where he had met her.

Thevenin rushes towards the stunned lady, "H-Hey! Get up!" he hassles at Zyra's critically weak state. "Now is not a time for you to melt here!" Thevenin reaches out his hand to motivate the injured lady into moving away from the disastrous flames.

"You were spreading yourself too thin... You wanted to save everyone, but you only got the chance to save me. You kept blaming yourself because other than us, no one made it alive that haunting night." Zyra rehearses, piercing Volt's stance.

"In fact, you were so devastated that you eventually gave up wearing any armor just because you thought you could be nimbler." Zyra continues to speak as Volt trembles. "T-That's not true..." he murmurs in denial.

"You would continuously visit this very garden for a reason. You were always seeking peace of mind because deep down, you never stopped blaming yourself for the accident." Zyra states, causing a small tear to grow on Volt's eyes.

"You never forgave yourself for failing. It's why you never spared a second for yourself... IYou even made a promise to yourself that this wouldn't happen again." the elaborating gatekeeper continues to speech.

"I'm here to remind you that I had lost everything *with you*. We share the same pain, Thevenin..." she sheepishly adds. "I have no doubts that you were always frustrated at me because, in a way, I was an obstacle in your path... But you saw something in me that no one else saw. You even trained me to become a gatekeeper so that we can stop chaos together, remember?" Zyra happily says.

"You trusted me to the point where you bestowed your own sword to me. Was it because you saw tremendous potential in me? Or was this because you never felt worthy to wield such a weapon? It didn't matter at the time... We constantly reminded each other that we'd have each other's backs no matter what..." Zyra finally concludes.

"That is, until death did us apart."

In angst, Volt takes a step back from Zyra. "We made an oath to save those around us, did we not? For those we lost that night, for those who have no means to protect themselves..." Zyra states. Volt continues to take another step back.

"Even if this whole void is sickening... I found out that your lack of cooperation is limiting our time..." Zyra eerily states. "I didn't want to accept it at all, but the prophet hasn't missed a single prediction... And if she states you're the reason why we're all going to perish, then it is my duty to honor the fallen and—" Zyra declares once again.

"Stop, Zyra." Volt interrupts. With sorrow written over his monstrous face, he coldly glares at the righteous gatekeeper. "...I don't want to be reminded whose side you chose." Volt mournfully states.

Zyra notices how distraught Volt became over the idea that he truly was alone. The burden of being a walking target continues to taint Thevenin's selfless promise. In no way does the target wish to carry his selfless promise after the whole world had turned on him. Was he foolish enough to hold onto his promise? Or did he believe abandoning his oath would liberate him of unwanted pain? Volt scurries in existential discomfort.

"...Heh, between you and Sympl, I can't tell who's worse at watching over my back." Volt quietly states as he wipes his tears with his warm arms. "I can't believe you've been brainwashed too." the tired Imporian remarks.

Without hesitating, Volt and his robotic companion turn around and march away from the relentless gatekeeper. "Last warning, Zyra. If you dare face me once more, I'm not going to hold back. I'm not going to forgive you for siding with that imp." Volt declares.

Still sparking electrical tidbits, Zyra finds herself isolated in the heating void. The disappearance of her comrades left behind blazing trails of hot air that begins to boggle her mind.

. . .

What were you thinking when you were harming yourself like that?

...

Don't you know how important blood is?

I do...

Then why did you hurt yourself like that, sweetheart?

To protect *my* blood.

Ophelia's bulky ears strike up. "Oh?" Ophelia questions surprisingly. "That's really impressive! Having family members with you in the void... Just wow! By probability, you two were never supposed to be united like this." the prophet adds.

The prophet finishes patching up Reza's slit arm as she then curls her claws through her hair to feel her rough strands of hair. "Amphy was never supposed to exist in the first place." Reza quietly states. Ophelia tilts her head at the young lady. "Really?" Ophelia questions giddily.

"...Thank you for patching me up." Reza responds in an attempt to cut the topic short. "What do you mean by wasn't supposed to exist in the first place?" Ophelia hashes the question again. "I'd rather not..." Reza jots.

"Well, if it makes you feel better, none of us truly were meant to wake up again." Ophelia begins to speech as she stops caressing Reza's hair. "We lived a beautiful life, died, and just when you thought you were going to walk the stairway of peaceful eternity, you get screwed over by a lot of factors." the prophet explains. "If anything, this is the opportunity to fight for your life, not forfeit it." she adds confidently.

Ophelia then jumps down from the stationed paintbrush. Upon landing, the prophet helps Reza stand up. She offers her talons which alerts Reza as this is the first time she focuses on Ophelia's hands. Hesitant, she gently takes Ophelia's glossy talons and stands up. This is also when Ophelia realizes how Reza towers over her. As the prophet scans the now patched-up guardian, she notices a huge slash on her stomach.

"Ouchie..." Ophelia whispers. "Did one of those faceless hunters hit you there?" the curious prophet asks. "You mean, Aphotic?" Reza, now more awake, replies. Reza continues, "Forget about it." – "Really, did Aphotic do this to you?" – "No..." – "Then who or what did this to you?" – "I already told you. *Amphy wasn't supposed to exist*." Reza coldly quotes.

"Once again, I appreciate your help in patching me up. However, I can't stay here and wait for Aphotic to come rolling by and hurt us." Reza declares as she reaches out her hand to the distracted Amphy.

Are you really scared of those useless hunters?

They're heartless scarf collectors. I'm not going to play with that.

And what if I told you there was a way to stop them for good?

I wouldn't believe you.

Sweetheart, are you aware that we're all running out of time?

I am aware...

And what are you going to do if you don't get the champion's scarf?

Champion's scarf...?

See, those hunters are amassing nasty people to get a magenta colored scarf.

Magenta dude...

They're doing this because the last one standing with that color wins the election, thus granting you another chance at happiness.

Does that make any sense to you?

Magenta dude and the leader of Aphotic...

Oh? Looks like you met our two trouble makers.

Both of them partially informed me of this.

Excited to hear that Reza has more awareness than expected, Ophelia giddily smiles at the bandaged guardian. "Looks like we might be on the same page then! How thrilling!" Ophelia remarks.

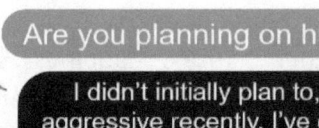

Are you planning on hurting magenta dude?

I didn't initially plan to, but he's been aggressive recently. I've only requested to take one of his appendages in exchange for another chance at happiness…

I ended up losing a hand… B-But it's okay! Nothing as bad as that scar you have.

Last time I checked, he was troubled by many.

I can imagine. Between the scarf and the parasite, he's been getting wilder as time goes on…

What do you mean parasite? Are you talking about those cables?

That thing on his back is gnawing his brains out. If it takes full control of its host, we may not have an opportunity to secure the champion's scarf.

That's too bad. Not my problem though.

It is! Aphotic is trying to handle the situation, but we can't let them take it first! We need to intercept them or we'll perish into nothingness!

Are you going to let that happen!?

I don't have the balls to deal with that again.

Would you do it for your child?

Alarmed at her words, Reza sinks her posture. The deaf boy gives the two ladies an odd look. "I…" Reza mutters in defeat. Reza gleams at Amphy who continues to quiver fearfully. Reza takes a few moments to organize her thoughts. Cooperation wasn't her thing – too many failures blunder her vision, yet her drive to continue stands in front of her. It shakes in fear, but that's because it knows what she must do. The young boy simply nods negatively, yet she understands his concerns.

"We!" Ophelia spouts, lifting Reza's head up. "I've been seeking out a champion to help me secure another chance at happiness, sweetheart. I promise that if you help me, we will share our precious rewards!" Ophelia cheeringly explains. Still doubtful, Reza ponders on what the prophet had been explaining. "This is all too sudden..." she proposes.

"Keep in mind that we don't have much time left either!" Ophelia continues to spout in hopes of clarifying the guardian's mind. "I just... I'm never going to be strong enough to protect my..." Reza cracks as she begins to sob. Seeing her tears trickle down her cheeks punctured a hole in the deaf boy's heart. "I-I just... I'm not ready to lose again..."

"Sweetheart! You have the heart of a champion! If we work together, we can absolutely stop all of those nasty monsters around us! I need you now!" Ophelia encourages.

The tone of the impish prophet bothers Reza. Empathic, yet persistent. This fusion of indirect demands causes Reza to ponder what the prophet truly desired. More specifically, it reminds Reza of a terrible time she had experienced with commanding people.

Reza sniffles through her tear-dripping face, "Face it..." Reza ruffles through her tears. Amused, Ophelia pays close attention to Reza's attitude. "You don't want to help *me*..." Reza scourges.

"No one *really* wants to help me..." Reza shrivels. "No one wants to help anyone with the burden of a child..." the sadden guardian then picks up her gigantic paintbrush with anger pouring through her veins. "Hell, why would anyone not take advantage of a stupid, hopeless mut like myself, huh?" Reza continues to say with visible frustration written over her face. Ophelia takes a step back in fear.

"You..." Reza points her paintbrush at Ophelia menacingly. "You're just like everyone else... And I can't trust people like you. How dare you continue to take advantage of the weak..." Reza speaks up. The prophet gets a bit jumpy when she sees this shift, "No, sweetheart... This is your last opportunity in changing the results of the election! If we win, you and Amphy will live forever without any more disturbances! I swear it!" Ophelia yelps.

Living forever? Have you lost your mind…?

The Astra is in danger and if we don't team up now, the next Astral vibration is going to kill all three of us!

And what the hell do you expect me to do about it!?

Lend me your body!

"My body…?" Reza mumbles in anger. Visions of nasty adults flash through her mind. Of course, how could Reza forgive herself after the first time she lent her body to a pulverous abuser? These thoughts trigger traumatic rage in her veins. "That's the last thing you'll ever have!" she coldly states before lifting her paintbrush against Ophelia. Upon rising the gigantic weapon over the impish prophet's head, Reza's eyes burst wide open in sharp pain.

"I declare you as my next champion… Whether you like it or not." Ophelia deviously says. Frozen, Reza could not bare to move her body out of an intense, cold pain. "Shh… Don't worry, the pain is temporary. It'll all be over soon…" Ophelia reassuringly states. The deafen Amphy looks over to see that Ophelia had dug her remaining talons into Reza's ribs, causing absolute distress.

Amphy screams loudly and runs away from the crazed duo. In his crazed sprinting, he drops the doll he once held ever-so tightly.

Before Reza could reach out her free hand towards the boy, the prophet shushes her. "Do not worry about the child. I told you that I am going to help you save him once we win the election." Ophelia eerily whispers. Reza suffocates from the penetrating claws. Essentially, Ophelia lets go of the guardian once her cracked claws had been implanted onto Reza's ribs.

"And now, you will understand my point of view." Ophelia declares to the unconscious body of Reza.

Chapter XIV:
Life Ad Mechanical Menaiety

Be grateful for what you have...

Void-Imporia gradually appears more shattered. Since the disappearance of the yellow ribbon, cracks and sharp slopes that rise through the ground have become more evident. Jogging in the vast void became perilous as the Imporian and his robotic backpacking companion took precautions to avoid any unnecessary punctures.

Volt takes a moment to rest up after his exhilarating escape from Aphotic's most recent ambush. Huffing, he begins to ease himself. The duo practically ran a marathon just to find themselves deeply lost in the colorless island. Now in private, the escapist clears his throat. "Sympl, you have some explaining to do." Volt says after catching his breath.

Tell me why you want to win the election.

I've never agreed to such an ambitious goal. I only want to make sure you're safe.

How full is your battery, Sympl?

As long as I'm with you, full!

You're very clingy for a robot, y'know?

Did our enemies impact you enough?

Depends on your definition of impact...
Do you believe my existence is the
reason why everyone is gone?

No evidence proves such statement against you. Perhaps
there are other forces in play other than yourself, however.

Man, you'd lie to me just to stay on my back, huh?

I am stating facts, Master Volt.

...Listen up carefully, I am going to
request just one favor from you, Sympl.

How may I serve you?

Zap me when I get too snappy, please?

"I do not believe in harming you, Volt." Sympl responds as his host begins to chuckle. "I'm sorry..." Volt says as he continues to laugh. "I've been so stupid recently!"

If Sympl had a neck, it'd tilt it in confusion. "I couldn't see this for a while now, but you're just looking out for my back." Volt chuckles. "I am currently doing that." Sympl puns. "I'd be really selfish of me to get hurt since we're in this together." Volt comments as he places his hands on his hips triumphantly. "From now on, we're going to prove to Zyra and all those other nasty people how we can save the void from those weird flaps in the sky!"

The Imporian cheerfully chuckles – "That being said, let's find the tallest mountain, no—let's make a huge tower! Yeah! Then we can punch that stupid star and it'll for sure leave everyone alone! Heck while we're at it, let's make sure it can bring back the whole island!" Sympl remains quiet upon listening to his comrade who lacks any logical brain cells.

"In theory, doesn't that equate to winning the election?" Sympl asks. Disturbed by the mention of the idea, Volt begins to huff. "Volt, according to all collected accounts from subject Ophelia, perhaps she has been hinting this too." Sympl argues.

"Garsh, we're really on the wrong foot with her, aren't we?" Volt rubs his head in anguish. "Perhaps if we continue to hide until all of our competitors are eliminated, we'd have an increased probability of winning." Sympl emits a happy-toned beep in response.

"Well, as long as we can wish everything back to normal, I think that'd be a good idea." Volt comments. Agreeing, the duo takes a few more steps deeper into the array of spikey hills in search for hiding locations. Promptly, the robot flares up and uses its signature warning alert, "Error detected!"

"Will we ever catch a break?" the flustered Imporian rambles to himself. From the distance, the duo could catch a glimpse of the forewarned silhouette. The escapist squints his eyes in order to identify what could have been nearby. He then makes a hasty conclusion after barely recognizing two pillar-like shapes.

Once he recognizes the gigantic paintbrush, he knew it had to be his only hero; the only person who had ever taken a stance to defend him from the persistent legion of Aphotic. "Sympl... Is that the lady who dresses up like the gatekeepers that saved us from Aphotic?" Volt asks with excitement in his throat. Sympl felt his contagious energy and beeped excitingly as well, "Loading... Reza identified! Indeed, it is! We should thank her for her assistance in our escape." Sympl suggests.

The two silently agree and begin to approach Reza from behind. With enough distance to not startle her, Volt softly clears his throat once again. "Um, hey there again…" the escapist stammers in hopes of not surprising his respected guardian.

"Uh, I'm sorry we got off on the wrong foot and all. I didn't know you were trying to help me earlier. So, yeah… Uh, thanks a lot for stopping those buffoons for me!" Volt awkwardly thanks. The guardian had clearly been listening to Volt's speech yet refuses to turn around and properly address him. "Did we ever formally introduce each other?" Volt nervously asks as he winces. The guardian releases a faint giggle and finally turns around to face Volt.

What in the name of Imporia did she become?

Startled, Volt uncontrollably jumps – the face he remembers did not align with what he was perceiving. "What the hell happened to you!?" Volt gracelessly spouts.

Immediately, he noticed that Reza's mouth is stitched shut. This flips Volt's stomach upside-down. "W-Who did this to you!?" the flinching Imporian questions as he couldn't maintain eye contact. "Sympl! Er—! Help her!" he impulsively demands.

The Imporian couldn't stop blurting words due to the sheer fear the guardian had induced onto him. Her faint giggling wickedly transforms into snickering. Reza winces and begins to lift up her hefty brush. Oddly confused, Sympl's tactical cables are rapidly drawn outwards as a reaction to Volt's terrified state. Reza sluggishly swings her weapon at the duo. Seeing this telegraphed attack, Sympl slips Volt out of harm's way.

"Target confirmed as a threat!" Sympl shrieks out. Reza tauntingly winces her eye and gives a devious smile upon hearing Sympl. "No! S-She's in a ton of pain, Sympl! We need to help her!" Volt's voice scrambles. The guardian continues to heavily swing her massive paintbrush at the jumbled duo. Evidently, the jumpy Imporian dodges all of her slow strikes. In one of her missed strikes, she demolishes an entire spike pillar just with the force of her paintbrush.

"She's crazy strong!" Volt yells. The duo finds themselves stuck dodging her ferocious pursuit. "If you want to help the target, perhaps we must liberate her of pain, Volt!" Sympl suggests. "Liberate!? How?" Volt frantically questions. The Imporian focuses on his footing to ensure he doesn't get smacked by the walloping paintbrush. "Take off the target's scarf!" Sympl states.

Volt's velvet scarf requires protection due to how risky their movements became. Sympl redirects its tactical wires to tightly wrap the loose flaps to each other. "If we don't take it off her first, she'll tear us apart!" the robot declares. The Imporian understood this predicament, but couldn't help seeing the guardian in agonizing pain. "We can't do that, Sympl! Otherwise, she'll melt like the Aphotic members!" Volt cries out with a guilty tone. The guardian's brutal attacks began to pick up speed.

"If you cannot do it, this unit can. Permission to yank off target's scarf?" Sympl coldly questions. Reza thrusts her paintbrush directly at the Imporian's neck. Instantly, he bends backward hoping that Sympl's cables would catch his fall. Volt underestimates this and falls on his back – Sympl's cables were too few and frail to hold his weight. The guardian crisply smirks as she spins her bulky staff onto the ground. The adrenaline-filled Imporian merely slips away, avoiding a ground-denting impact.

"I can't... I can't answer that!" Volt sheepishly cries out. The persistent guardian tosses her weapon in the air and catches it by the thickest edge. She then aims the free sharpened tip at her target and begins to blindly strike the Imporian. The multiple jabs thrown at Volt were misdirected by the fury of cables Sympl flailed. Random strikes punctured and tore away bits of Sympl's cables, decreasing its functionality.

With cables being shred apart, Sympl begins to lose control of its movements. The loose ends of the cables spur bits of electricity and hot sparks. "What about you agreeing to outlive the competitors?" Sympl questions. "I don't know, Sympl! We're running out of options! Let's just escape!" Volt yelps from the middle of the assault. "Take off the target's scarf or we're going to be deleted!" the robot furiously argues.

Volt catches the paintbrush, halting Reza's movements. Sympl then aggressively wiggles what little control it had over the cables in order to clap its wires together. The robot then proceeds to eject most of its armed wires. Consequently, this causes a discharge to travel through the cables, lashing out a searing spout of electricity directly at Reza.

With an eruption of paralyzing heat, the guardian flinches and pulls back her stance. "Now, Volt! Pull the scarf!" Sympl demands with a glitchy voice. With full indication of Reza's vulnerability and no more time to hesitate, the Imporian realizes how Sympl gave up its own defense mechanism to slow her down. Volt gets up and sprints with all of his might. He latches his hand onto her scarf's loose flap and proceeds to mightily yank her scarf.

Reza's scarf refused to come off.

Despite the grand force Volt had yank with, he only ended up tugging her scarf and accidentally releases the loose cloth. The Imporian did tear part of her ragged skin, but this is only the because Reza's scarf had been stitched into her neck. The Imporian remains speechless once he discovers how her scarf had been integrated into her skin.

A pained snicker muffles through Reza's tearful face. She bursts out of the paralyzed state and with every ounce of force she had, she swung directly at Volt. Before the Imporian could even react, Sympl unlatches its last cable from Volt and desperately springs itself into the air. The brutal swing was blocked by the robotic projectile.

As soon as the hefty paintbrush crashes into Sympl, the robotic companion explodes into pieces. The absolute obliteration of Sympl causes an electrical explosion to discharge around the nearby environment. Ultimately, its robotic shell crumbles and scatters in front of the floored Imporian.

"S-Sympl!" Volt screeches after seeing battered metallic scraps on the colorless floors. The broken core of the robotic shell pours grey oils, thick fumes, and feisty sparks.

Without the burden of his companion perching on his back, the Imporian feels weightless. However, with the sacrifice of his only friend daunting him, he could not bare to lift his spirits. The guardian had been completely paralyzed as a result of the counter-attack. She stood as frozen as the Imporian's expression.

"S-Sympl…" Volt tears up. Materialistic or not, the monstrous Imporian's attachment to his partner in crime tore him apart. How could he have been so ignorant to treat mere objects with abuse? Regret, resentment, and sorrow fills his hollow heart. "N-No! Sympl, this isn't what I meant!" Volt cracks, enabling sobbing in his tone.

"You…! You have no idea what you've done!" Volt angrily engrosses, making his fangs erect a bit longer than usual. "You're going to—" the pissed Imporian boils up until he looks at all the damage he's done to Reza.

Nothing – or rather, no visible difference. Reza was completely unaffected by Sympl's electrical explosion. A simple minor burnt hand and a shocked state was visibly apparent.

The petrified Imporian gradually gathers up the courage to stand up. Reza's bleeding stitched scarf had been untouched – intact from before the robot's sacrifice. The Imporian's impossible task of unscarfing the stitched monster grows demoralizingly. In the complete silence, Reza's muffled voice shimmers. Volt sees that the stitches around Reza's lips had been slightly looser than usual. "Free…" her quiet voice coldly says.

The Imporian's eyes open widely upon hearing her stammer. "F-Free… m… me…" the guardian's faint voice struggles to breathe. Suddenly, the stitches around her lips shut tightly as she begins to emit an ominous snickering sound.

"Alright, time to shut up, *Heartbreak*." a familiar voice echoes. In sheer awe, Volt recognizes the voice as none other than Ophelia's. "O-Ophelia!?" Volt shouts. "Long time no see, Champion! Well, you can't really see my beauty this time, can you?" the voice ominously echoes.

Ticked off, Volt rapidly scans his eyes around the spikey fields to see if he could spot the prophet. "How cute, you miss me that much that you're trying to see me again, huh? Well, don't bother, searching for me – you won't be able to see me anyway." Ophelia giggles.

Reza's body continues to fight for movement, yet the ominous voice of Ophelia hushes her. "You like my new puppet? She's extremely persistent about taking your scarf, y'know?" Sick to his stomach, Volt continues to gawk at the twitching, stitched figure.

"Ophelia... What the hell have you done to her?" – "Bah, you can't assume I'm this unhinged! Mommy wanted to save her son and needed a little bit of help from someone who knows how to end your pathetic life!" Ophelia's non-center voice thunders psychopathically.

"Ahahaha! And now, without your stupid metallic parasite bugging me off every five seconds, looks like you're completely useless!" Ophelia uncontrollably snickers. Volt trembles in total fear. What could she have possibly done to unlock this power?

Volt's mind races parabolically between the thoughts of an impending doom and how he could even muster this impossible challenge. Minuscule movements around Reza's body began to tense up. Her incredibly slothful movement was feasible; however, she makes a futile effort to extend her arm. With her burnt hand in the scratched paintbrush, the guardian aims her next strike at Volt.

"Oh? Looks like mommy still wants to keep on fighting for her little boy, right!?" Ophelia teases. Relentless tears trickle down Reza's only eye. It was at that moment where Volt comprehended their intentions.

The Imporian briefly glares at Reza's sorrowful expression only to get distracted by her finally striking down at him. Volt uproars and grabs the paintbrush again, this time without any cables assisting him. Her weak swing wasn't strong enough to create any type of indentures this time around.

Volt then wraps a leg over the staff and reaches for the brush itself. He feels Reza regaining full movement due to subtle vibrations she was producing. In an attempt to disarm her of the weapon, he tries to pull the bulky staff out of her grip. Unfortunately, he ends up slipping yet again, but latches his hands onto the hairs of the weapon.

Still pulling away, he ends up plucking the brush portion away from the weapon. Upon doing so, Reza violently shakes him off of the now brushless metallic staff. Said brush flew off into the spikey field without trace.

The now brushless staff reveals to have a hollow hole within it. Reza instantly notes this since she felt her weapon become more lightweight. The guardian flips the staff and tucks her hand deep inside the hollow staff, holding it like a javelin.

During her discovery, Volt disheartened notices Sympl's shattered body which leaked grey oils. Additionally, the robot had been shooting hot sparks and searing fumes, making the Imporian take a cautious approach.

Without any breathing space, Reza's body dashed towards Volt as if she teleported. Upon reaching him, she thoughtlessly jabs him with her new javelin. Reza's mind aims to miss, yet Ophelia's control redirects the jab at the dead center of his neck. The combination of this results in piercing Volt's shoulder pad.

The sting was so rapid and intense that it blew him away into the distance. Volt's tense body crashes into the sidelines of spikey pillars. What felt like sheer luck, he avoids getting impaled by the surrounding's broken pillars. With his eyes semi-closed, he notices that his wrecked shoulder pad had red stains splattered. Was this his blood or the effect of the red-wrapped javelin? Once a drop of red hits his lavish velvet scarf, he feels a slight burn.

Just near his resting position was the missing brush. "C'mon, Champion! I thought you were going to put up a fight!" Ophelia's insidious voice sings around. The slight burn he felt reminds him of Blank's bleeding pin-arms clashing with Sympl's tactical wires.

To this, Volt snags the brush and makes a mad dash out of his current position as he sees Reza's body being flung towards him. He spot's Sympl's oily body and runs at it without hesitation. Once he carefully reaches the bot's broken state, he uses the brush to soak up the grey oils like a sponge.

He then glances at Reza who is spotted running towards him at full speed. With her javelin aimed outwards, she pokes at Volt who sprung away from the attack. Her new configuration was faster than lifting a heavy paintbrush which allowed her to conduct a follow-up attack. The Imporian's weightlessness helped him dodge her devastating blows.

With the two at their peak of nimbleness; they charge into each other with their weapons poking outwards. The two competitors had jousted each other as they cross paths.

Paused from their extensive strikes, the guardian manages to rip off one of the Velvet scarf's flaps. In exchange, the Imporian had successfully achieved to paint parts of Reza's red scarf in a greasy grey color.

In the portions that stained her scarf, the guardian feels an excruciating burn surround her body. Colorful particles begin to burst out of her entire body – Reza initiated the sequence of evaporation. "Shh! Why does that burn!? *Venti!* Why is our puppet burning up!?" Ophelia's echo disturbingly shouts.

Volt pants heavily once he witnesses yet another person suffer a melting farewell. Reza's body refuses to be defeated as she eagerly ties the stolen velvet scarf around her neck. Upon seeing this, Volt's heart sunk – Reza's evaporation process stops once she proudly wears the velvet scarf.

"Finally! Yes, finally! After all this time, it's mine! It's finally mine! I've acquired a velvet scarf!" Ophelia celebrates as she uncontrollably exhorts a burst of deranged laughter. "Mother Reza! Time to kill two birds with one stone, will ya'?" Ophelia's violent snicker spreads like wildfire.

The torn Reza menacingly marches towards the shocked Imporian. Her ferocious steps grew into weak trudging. The glowing magenta appendage gracefully wrapped around Reza's neck gives her a level of resistance – as if she felt the machinations of freedom racing through her heart. Suddenly, Ophelia's control over her aching body weakens.

Eventually, she falls on her knees and slips out of her javelin. "Get up! You have enough fuel left, dammit!" Ophelia's ominous voice faintly screeches. Prone to any attack, Volt stutters in his movement. The stitches that once shackled her red scarf with her skin were loosening up by the moment. Could this have been because of her new color taking over? Is this what Ophelia struggles on maintaining? He debates whether this is the perfect opportunity to unscarf her or even something else. Something much more painful than a violent tug.

Volt melancholically stares at the loose javelin. "I'm not going to let you go now!" Ophelia's voice scatters once again. Hearing her voice bellow suddenly makes the cursed stitches attempt to retighten itself. Seeing this creepily occur, Volt picks up the heavy javelin. He then trembles as he knows what must be done. His heart pounds loudly, his throat grows dry, and his palms begins to sweat. "I'm sorry!" Volt sorrily shouts as he swings the tip of the javelin between the small free space near Reza's neck.

After the swing, he opens his eyes in suspense. His swift and accurate swinging had indeed torn the stitches out of Reza's neck. To this, Reza's red-to-grey and velvet scarf were completely loose. The Imporian hesitantly reaches out his hand only for her to slap his wrist away.

With the leftover energy Reza had, she accumulates all of her lingering will and desperately attempts to go for an unscarf. Reza places her battered hands on the cursive scarf and grips it without holding back a single ounce of energy. Volt's eyes lit up when she finally yanks the scarf successfully. The metallic javelin drops on the ground with a heavy ringing thud.

Reza had yanked her own scarf.

"What the hell are you doing!?" Ophelia's echo screeches. Her echoing voice grows silent to the point where her presence simply faded away upon Reza's release. The faint mumbling of her voice could no longer be heard by anyone in the nearby field. The field's silence was quickly swarmed with the rush of the piping steam jolting out of Reza's body.

And then, Reza's torn body crashes onto the floor. Volt quickly drops onto the ground to collect her fallen body. The tiara she wore cracks and other decoratives begin to scatter away from her body. "H-Hey! You're melting!" Volt stutters in surprise. All of Reza's stitches were undone and evaporated before the rest of her body phased out.

She gracefully holds out the palms of her heating hand and places it on Volt's flustered cheek. "N-none of this is y-your fault..." she faintly whispers. Reza's body struggles to maintain form as the steam her body produces burns like a wildfire. "Forget about that! Save your energy!" Volt prowls as he begins to shed a tear.

"Magenta dude..." she gracefully whispers as her voice continues to grow ever weaker. "Shut up! Put the scarf back on you! It's the only way you'll save yourself!" Volt scrambles as he attempts to place the recaptured cloth on her slit neck. Reza weakly slaps his hand away from her neck.

"Hey! What the hell do you think you're doing!? Let me help you, please!" Volt cries out once again. "Magenta dude, use that gift to save those in need... D-Don't waste your time..." Reza barely pronounces.

Waste my time!? Dammit, Reza! Stay with me! I can't afford to lose another friend — not like this! Please! Take the damn scarf already! I need you!

Reza's dissipating body releases a dim giggle, "W-We really *do* wear the s-same shoes after all..." The faint Reza gently closes her eyes upon hearing his soft barking. "I'm so sorry, Magenta dude... B-But this husk isn't Reza's anymore..." she weakly mutters.

"Bull-crap! I'm not going to let you go now!" Volt pitches as he forces the scarf over her melting neck again. "How sweet... But if I s-stay, *she* will win..." Reza exerts. Once again, Reza uses her last bits of energy to remove the velvet scarf off of her gaping neck.

"It's o-okay… Promises aren't meant to be b-broken, right…?" Reza struggles to say. Her shattering words were not understandable at this point, but the persistent Imporian hears enough to conclude her prompt. "I promise this isn't the end! We're going to find a way out of this mess, I swear!" Volt spasms.

"…D-Do me a solid and k-keep your promises…" she adds, smirking at the sad Imporian. More colorful streams burst out of multiple pours of her body. She sends off the Imporian with a gentle glint. She barely opens her mouth one last time, "A-And please… P-Protect… Amphy…" Her last words bittersweetly rung in the ears of the Imporian.

She delicately transforms her defeated expression into a gentle wince. Ultimately, her physical form reaches its peak limit then shatters into infinite particles that flow away into the invisible air.

Volt flinches upon first-handedly witnessing her burst into dark particles. He loses his balance and falls over his crouching position. Once he faceplants onto the cold floors of Void Imporia, he remains grounded and unleashes quiet sobbing.

How could he be so careless? Why did he have to see this unfold in front of him? Why did Sympl do something so stupid? Thoughts raced around his clouded head – perhaps he was ultimately wrong about himself. Should he dare continue wearing the magnet scarf around his neck?

His sobbing spirals louder and more maniacal – no voice to cheer him up, no reminders to clear his mind, nothing to undo the consequences he has permanently written. His heart pounces rapidly and his face grew pale. In efforts to stabilize his breathing pattern, he slowly opens his tear-induced eyes to a sight that disrupts his train of thought.

And then it hit him – Volt violently quivers. With the loss of his robotic companion and an innocent mother who wished for happiness, the Imporian angrily stares at a set of cracked red claws. These claws weren't always red, but evidently remarked stains of blood – Reza's blood to be precise. The massive tears that fell on his cheeks began to halt as he dreadfully locks his sight at the glowing talons.

Still focused on the impish claws, his trembling figure gradually stands up. He then gently hovers his foot over them. Instantly, he fiercely stomps over the claws, shattering them like glass.

Over. And over. And over. And over. And over. And over again.

The Imporian coldly continues to repeatedly stomp until the claws became a pile of mashed ashes. The frequency of each thwomp gets faster as the Imporian begins to violently pant. His rage could've easily evaporated his own tears. Even when the talons were disintegrated to nothing, he continues to bash his foot until he could no longer channel his internal pain.

Out of sheer frustration, he releases a roar that echoes through the devoided island. This violent screech catches the attention of all remaining survivors, as if he produced his own astral vibration.

Upon venting, he takes silent moments to reflect what has occurred. Before he leaves the haunting fields, Volt reclaims the fallen piece of the velvet scarf the atrocious Reza had claimed. As he walks away, he sees Sympl's broken shell, bends over and places his palm on its hot surface. "Sympl..." Volt unsteadily says to himself. "You've always had my back..."

"I... Thanks to you, I know what finally must be done..." Volt winces. The disheartened Imporian notices how his partner's decimated body continues to flicker a weak light from its lens. He releases a heavy, uneasy sigh. Knowing that a part of Sympl stares back at him, the Imporian clears his throat.

"...Permission to shut down granted, buddy. You did amazing..." his voice cracks. The steaming robotic shell stops sparking. Any remaining bickering lights within the bot zoned into darkness, completely arresting the remaining life it had. Volt exhales deeply before he gets up one more time.

He flees the daunting battlefield begrudgingly. Volt makes his way into the colorless horizons of Void Imporia. Only then would his plan concur.

Time's coming to an end.

Chapter XV:
Living-Dead Promises

Promises can't be broken...

In his recovering state, Blank rests on his back and gazes at the astral twin-tied ribbon from the roofless arena. "It's so close, yet so far away." Blank coughs. The curious masked maiden gently pets the leader of Aphotic. "Mister Blank..." Viola hesitantly speaks up.

I regret to tell you this, but the Astra's red ribbon isn't healthy. We still haven't secured our target.

Nonsense, Aphotic will end this once and for all!

Blank, Aphotic is dead.

...We still have Zoriadia, you and myself. That's enough to keep the dream alive, Viola.

Zoriadia hasn't returned since the last Astral vibration. We have no other options left than to—

I-I can still fight! No need for you to interfere!

You cannot even stand on your own two feet.

S-Shut up! I can and will end this once and for all!

Mister Blank, I am realistically your only option left.

If it's not necessary, we don't need accidents now.

We've talked about it a million times now! When are you going to let me stop the void master?

Let Zoriadia handle it! She's a gatekeeper, she can do it!

Stop projecting Zoriadia onto that gatekeeper.

...

Visiting the forsaken battlefield, the prophet silently bends over where Reza's body evaporated. She gently scavenges the rippled grounds in search of her detached claws. In seeking her remote hand, the prophet gazes at the shattered robot. Glimpsing at Volt's lost partner cracks a smirk on her face. Ophelia snickers vigorously, celebrating the elimination of the champion's best defense.

"The parasite is gone! Champion will no longer be a threat! Ahahaha!" Ophelia merrily cackles to herself. Her head starts to jiggle a bit. "So, what if poor Reza didn't stop him? She was way too resistive anyway!" Ophelia responds.

"You did an amazing job, Venti!" Ophelia continues to chant to herself. A nearby mumble occurs, causing Ophelia to carefully examine the broken bot once more. "Oh? You hear metallic scrapping...?" she speaks to herself.

"I-Impossible. All that work for nothing!? No, Sympl is dead. No denying it!" Ophelia jots to herself as the subtle metallic scrapping noise she mentions draws closer.

In her selfish victory, she finds a mystical pile of red powder. She joyfully ponders over the mysterious article to gradually realize that she had been staring at a familiar body part – a pair of smashed claws. She releases a sigh and concludes her scavenger hunt. "...Looks like we have to rely on old tactics again, huh?" Ophelia talks to herself again. Despite accepting that her talons were mushed into mesmerizing ashes, she gets distracted by a louder version of the metallic scrapping sound.

Paranoid, Ophelia scans the area again to spot where this sound was coming from. It was impossible for Sympl's thrashed metals to make such a sound, so where did it come from?

Her gawking widens once she spots the origin of the noise from afar. The gatekeeper heartlessly drags her sword across the rough grounds, simultaneously sharpening its edge. With an optimistic attitude, Ophelia relaxingly redirects her direction over to the silent survivor.

"Woah! Long time no see! Where are you going?" Ophelia cheerily asks. Her warm excitement intends to invite Zyra into a conversation, but the gatekeeper ignores her giddy voice and focuses on the void ahead of her. "Hey!" Ophelia bellows selflessly. Once again, Zyra neglects to pay any attention to the prophet.

The impish prophet then impulsively chases down Zyra. She then playfully knocks her shoulder pad with her broken hand to grasp the gatekeeper's attention. Zyra tensely turns around and gives Ophelia an uncomfortable, bitter glare.

The unsteady prophet felt sweat trickle down her neck upon receiving the freezing glare. Ophelia sturdily withstands Zyra's ridicule with an anxious smile. Her winced brows and lowered ears soften more than her sweet voice.

Regardless of the hollow glare, Ophelia shrugs it off with one of her goofy smiles. Clearly, Zyra must've been in need for some good news, right? "Champion!" Ophelia jubilantly cries out in an attempt to knock out Zyra's cold glare.

The prophet proceeds to deliver amazing news.

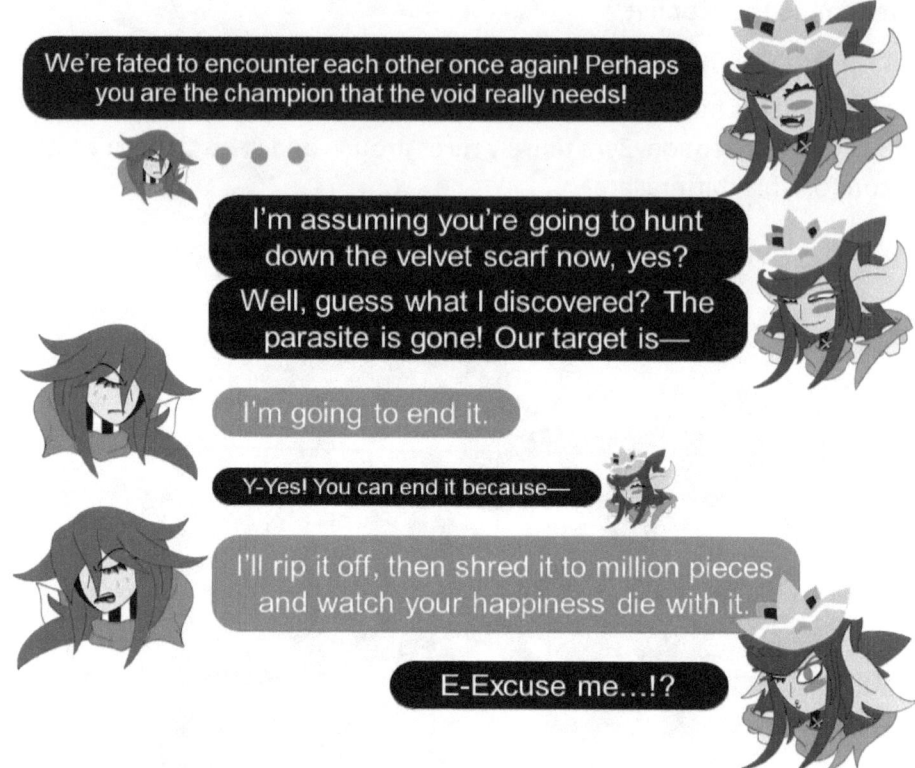

Uneasy, Ophelia stutters in wording. "Another chance at happiness? That's just a fantasy." Zyra boldly spews before disappearing into the void. Ophelia swipes her hand to catch Zyra but misses once she is reminded that she is clawless. Lashed by the gatekeeper's threat, the false prophet remains speechless and inanimate.

It didn't matter if Zyra was still recovering from the paralyzing shot – between her rebellious arrogance against the prophet's wishes and the lack of talons, the prophet begins to think that she may have no one to rely on anymore.

. . .

Roaming in silence, the Imporian carries the weight of his losses. His mind boggles with the anxieties of being completely alone. The inability to express himself ills him. The guilt of releasing the guardian from her scarf floods his boggled mind. "Is this my fault or not?" he echoes to himself. With no one to respond to his doubts, Volt remorsefully travels the void.

In his aimless marathon, Volt hears weeping. It was distant and faint enough to be mistaken for sounds running in his head. One thing for sure was that it was not being produced by him. He takes moments to realize this as he erects his posture upon grasping the fact that he was hearing distraught sounds. In search for where the voice could have possibly come from, he scans the area and follows the weeping until it becomes wailing.

To this, the Imporian reaches a deep sinkhole. Tectonic spikes stuck out forming a spiral set of ladders. In the absolute center of the underground tower lies a grim garden. "No way..." the Imporian mumbles to himself. He drops flat on his stomach to get a better view of the garden. He recalls and confirms that this indeed was the very same garden he had awoken from.

Filled with nostalgia, the Imporian decides to investigate his roots. However, he hesitates on going down due to his previous endeavors on escaping. "Hey Sympl, can we use your tactical cables to climb out of here like we did..." Volt's brightened tone hustles to one of mourning upon realizing he was alone. "Right..." he mumbles in defeat.

Volt jogs in place – he did feel as light as a feather and the spiraling stair-case structure encourages him to take a dive. His tiny peak of excitement forces him to precariously skip down the set of sharp plates. Once he swiftly reaches the bottom floor of the sinkhole, Volt examines the leafless tree. The hollow husk stands tall and lifeless, yet the once grey grass and wounded flowers flourished in blue, green, and yellow colors.

The Imporian runs his eyes around the large bark before getting startled by a muted whimper. With no 'error detected' alerts, Volt jolts his head around and spots a young boy huddling to himself. The frightened boy repulsed himself from Volt's unfamiliar figure. Having fin ears, fangs, and cloth that overlapped his attire must've scared the child. Amphy whimpers louder and clenches himself tighter upon seeing this.

Volt observes how the youngster is drenched in a bloody red scarf and even has some stains written on his face. His makes Volt feel uneasy, especially since the boy was sobbing. Did this boy fall in the hole and got hurt? Is he crying because he's trapped? The Imporian's mind races with these questions. Regardless of whatever pain the boy may be going through, the Imporian relates to him. He softens up and exerts an empathetic expression.

His attempt at calming the young boy grew pointless since the young boy trembles violently. The boy's gestures remind Volt that he masks the appearance of a fabled monster. "Am I really the monster here...?" the Imporian gloomily asks himself.

Amphy's closed attitude provokes haunting questions to the lonely Imporian. Volt deeply sighs and tries his best to ignore the negativity of the boy. He couldn't help knowing that someone new was still roaming in the void.

He resumes observing the towering tree. He gently places his hand on the trunk and closes his eyes. He then remembers his countless naps, deranged thoughts, and chats with his robotic companion.

Volt cracks a small smile when recalling these deep thoughts. Yet, the bittersweet recollection of his memories saddens him. He feels a drop of liquid on his head as if a raindrop had pelted him. He puzzlingly opens his eyes and feels another wet drop hit him. The Imporian then stares upwards and everything freezes. His entire world stays absolutely still for a brief moment.

The tree's shape... Why did it strike resemblance?

Volt then locks his eyes at Amphy. "Why are you hiding here?" Volt questions to the sheepish Amphy. Amphy does see the monster's mouth open and close as if there was a prompt being stated. However, the child still hears cluelessness and doesn't know how to gather a proper response. To this, Volt takes a step closer to Amphy, freaking him out.

He carefully analyzes Amphy precautious. "Where have I seen that headpiece before...?" he questions to himself, half-heartedly expecting an answer. Still petrified in fear, Amphy attempts to protect himself by placing his arms over his head. He then dashes over to the tree and attempts to wrap his arms on the branches as if he were to hug the tree.

Volt then shifts his eyes from Amphy's scared positioning to the elegant, yet withered tree. "There's no way…" he says to himself. As if lightning had struck him – he comprehends, without a doubt in his bones, that the young boy indeed was the son of Reza.

Upon his discovery, Volt takes the loose magenta strap that had fallen from his battle with Reza. He cautiously approaches Amphy and just when he gets close to him, he plants his knees to the ground.

Honoring Reza's promise, Volt holds out the loose scarf. Amphy recoils towards the tree when he sees the Imporian bending over. The young boy then calms down when he learns that there are no intentions of harm in the garden.

"Hey… This is yours." Volt gently spoke. The Imporian then poises the loose scarf at the shy boy.

The young boy reluctantly ends up picking up the magenta scarf. He then gives Volt a resentful look. "It's okay, really! In fact, let me help you out, buddy." Volt cheerfully pronounces knowing that the boy would not answer his conversation. The Imporian cautiously ties the scarf around the boy's neck and with that – Amphy had been wearing the scarf of a champion.

"It works…?" The Imporian questions once he sees how pompously the youngster wears a portion of the fabled velvet scarf. "Heh, you're looking like a champ…" Volt sighs. With five loose appendages wrapped around his neck, he gracefully holds onto them for a mere moment. "That means—" he whispers to himself before Amphy tugs his shirt.

"I-I'm scared…" the deaf boy oddly mumbles. Enthralled that Amphy did in fact say something, Volt gives him a strong smile with a whimsical chuckle. "Mister… Can you help me find mommy?" Amphy shudders quietly. The sorrow-filled words shook Volt's core. "H-Huh?" Volt trembles with a dry throat. "I-I… I ran away again and I'm scared she's hurt!" Amphy blurts with glossy eyes.

"I… I want to go home with Reza and Mister Poo!" the child painfully adds, penetrating Volt's heart with a spear of remorse.

Volt silently stands still as he soaks up the boy's lament. The Imporian's lips dehydrate and his eyes begin to grimace. "Please! Can you save Reza? Can you save her just like how the gatekeepers did back in the island? Just like when father got out his belt? Can you please save us? Please...?" Amphy's deafened and distraught voice cracks into Volt's stern stance.

He gathers no answers. How could he face this young boy's flooding eyes and break him apart with words? In silence, the Imporian takes a deep breath.

"Little man..." Volt softly speaks up. In his crouched position, he places his tainted hands on the boy's bushy hair. Volt exhales slowly and reveals a gentle smile. The gatekeeper hesitates on announcing special instructions to the troubled child. But with a focused gleam, there was one correct answer he thought about.

"...Stay here, okay?" he softly says. Utter silence fills the garden to the point where only the sounds of Amphy's sniffling could be heard. "That scarf you wear will help you reunite yourself with Reza. All you have to do is stay here until the time is right." Volt calmly adds.

Hearing his calming words astounds the youngster. Is there truly hope to be reunited? With the ensuing silence, Amphy could clearly hear the Imporian. "I promise to make Imporia safe again! Once this is all over, I'll come back and show you how beautiful the island is, okay?" Volt cheers on, capturing Amphy's complete attention.

"P-Promise...?" Amphy questions once more. The towering Imporian shakes himself and confidently delivers his reply. "I promise!" he jubilantly declares.

With the integrity of protecting what is left, the Imporian moves towards the ascending spikes. Amphy sees the determined Imporian heading towards the arching tectonics spikes that erect themselves out of the sinkhole. Volt performs a mighty jump and is able to start his escape out of the sinkhole. He then rushes through the spiraling staircase, leading him out of the now colorful garden. Before springing out of the sinkhole, Amphy watches the Imporian flee with a smile on his face.

Chapter XVI:
Yielding Event Horizon

The zombie, the witch, and the mysterious unbroken stitch...

After a long period of time, Void Imporia had seen its better days. The vast island that was once plain and empty was now scattered with spikes and cracks all over the colorless areas.

The Imporian final arrives at his desired destination - Aphotic's arena. Standing in the entrance causes Volt's heart to heavily pound. The chiseled arena towers over him menacingly, belittling his confidence. He holds himself together, yet ponders on other ideas. "Should I really do this? I mean, I could just wait outside... Erg—I can't hesitate either! Or can I...?" he thinks to himself.

His body quivers, his stomach is full of butterflies and his face flushes pale. The Imporian stands still. He scans the void behind him to see just that – a blank plain of nothingness. No digital advice, no mysterious malicious speeches, no heroic encounters. It was just the lofty arena and his unreleased thoughts.

The Imporian knew what had to be done. With the little courage he collects, Volt barges his way into the open arena. He emerges himself into the hollow coliseum and finds two figures resting at the lower-leveled bleachers. The masked man, who had focused on the melting red ribbon, notes the Imporian's invading presence.

Continuing to lock his direction at the Astra, Blank snickers. "When an appendage dies, it rolls up in the shape of a petal. Have you ever noticed that is starting to look like a flower?" Volt halts his movements for a moment. In this moment, Volt glances at the sky to observe how much the Astra has truly changed. He remains silent, mostly out of fear. "...I'm talking to *you*, monster boy." the masked man snaps.

"I'm curious to know if you're truly a monster or some artificial Imporian." Blank comments, facing his target that fashioned multiple flaps of magenta. Volt barely opens his mouth, ready to answer, then stops himself. "Mister Blank, please, wait!" Viola cries out. Blank then slothfully stands up and hunches over Viola. Here, Volt notices the bandages Blank had on his shoulder. "Viola, stay out of this! This is your final warning." the masked man grits before facing the Imporian.

You're the one who attacked me first! You owe me an apology!

You have some serious balls to come back and invade my arena again, strawberry.

Forget about it, plate face. Just tell me where Zyra is!

The audacity. You lack some serious manners, you hear?

You want manners? Okay, let's try this again. Can you answer my question? *Pretty please?*

For an intruder, you're extremely foolish.

Look, I get it. You're hurt that I'm not here for you. It's okay to be jealous sometimes, right?

Hah, you want to hear a really funny joke?

Shoot your shot, big boy.

Zoriadia being alive.

...?

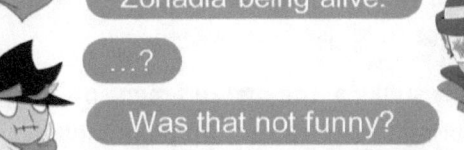

Was that not funny?

Whose Zory-ah-de-ha?

Forget about it — your gatekeeper friend is probably dead like everyone else.

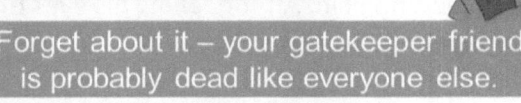

I wouldn't count on that!

Volt directs his face away from the masked man. Did he attribute to this massive loss? Despite the harassing commentaries, he couldn't help but feel guilty for all of the hunters who laid their lives over their questionable quest.

"They were all damned from the start anyways. Every single last one of them. Including Zoriadia." Blank murmurs. It becomes apparent that Volt's guilt slowly increases as Blank mentions his legion. Yet, his ears poke upon hearing the masked man's next statement. "Those pawns... You'd be impressed how much you're able to influence hopeless grunts when you sell them a fantasy." Blank adds with clarity in his voice.

"P-Pawns?" – "They were all stepping stones for this very moment, strawberry." Blank replies with his spreading smirk. "Their sacrifices are not in vain. After all, you *are* giving me my last opportunity to take what's so desperately mine." Blank smirks as he launches his pin arms into action. In the distance, a subtle marching could be heard. This did not distract Blank or Volt's impending showdown.

High above, there was yet another intruder who has been observing the entire conversation. She did not draw anyone's attention and remained well hidden. With the lack of functioning claws to grapple onto anything, she cautiously eavesdrops the two competitors getting near each other. Her disturbing frown widens once she sees the masked man rushing himself towards the Imporian. Defenseless and without reliable assistance from his robotic companion, Ophelia could smell her plan crumbling to pieces.

Logistically, she was worried on how she could stop a magenta-colored Blank of all people, but was also dying to see Volt lose his scarf once and for all. To Blank's rushing attack, Volt hesitantly takes a few steps back and anxiously tucks his loose flaps to himself.

With the prophet keenly stalking, the masked man sprinting at his target, and the Imporian preparing to embrace sharp pain, Viola places her hands over her face out of panic. A loud, meaty clash bursts in the center of the arena. Yet, Volt feels no pain. After opening his eyes from flinching, Volt sees a gatekeeper blocking Blank's attack.

The metallic sword slashes across the bleeding blades.

"Outta' my way!" the cold-hearted gatekeeper blurts before pushing Blank away with raging force. Without warning, she stylishly points her sharpened blade at Volt's neck. "Zyra!" Volt spouts in relief, baffling her stance with his excitement. Blank yelps in agony as his red pins grew darker. The cut that Zyra had indented onto him caused enough pain for Blank to hold back his attack.

He briefly composes himself only to fall short by hunching. "Zoriadia! Get out of my damn way!" Blank announces only for Zyra to coldly glares at Blank. "That's *my* target." she replies. The masked man releases tricky breathing, not believing what the gatekeeper had announced. "Square up." Zyra shouts at Volt.

Without hesitation, the Imporian's dreadful expression swung into joy. He even begins to chuckle out of comedy. This flaunts Zyra's sword-holding pose.

"I said square you, fool!" Zyra bellows. Volt continues to chuckle uncontrollably. He eventually cools down and begins to speak.

You're here... You're finally here! I'm so happy that you're finally here!

What is the meaning of this?

I finally understand! You came here to watch out for my back!

I wouldn't dare help a filthy monster like you.

Hahaha! You're completely right, Zyra! I am a monster! Why haven't I noticed sooner?

Stop laughing, creep!

Stop laughing? Hahaha! I can't do that! That'd make ole' Thevenin really sad again, right?

Don't you dare mention his name in vain, freak.

We're both wrong! It was all just a misunderstanding this whole time, Zyra!

What are you talking about?

I finally understand what truly needs to be done! And you're here to prove it!

Hold still, bucko! You're too late to think you can do anything to stop me!

I can never stop you, Zyra! That's why I want to cherish what you stand for!

H-Huh!?

Without hesitation, he tears off one of his loose flaps. Zyra sees his quick motion – before she could react, Volt gives her his brightest smile. Even with the guise of a monster, she sees a perfect reflection of her lost partner in crime.

Zyra recoils as a reaction. Before she could break out of her sudden daze, Volt had wrapped the loose appendage onto her. She then realizes that she now fashions a portion of the velvet scarf. Granting her the status of a champion, Zyra shutters in conflict.

Perplexed that she now wears a velvet scarf, she eases her fierce pose. The same cursive color that has ruined what she had been fighting against is suddenly overwhelming her with a sense of... *reunion*. Did she profoundly remember Thevenin's parting gift? Or was she enraged at her confusion?

Her cheeks become rosy, her eyes grew soft, and her breathing intensifies. She begins to see Volt's contagious smile yet combats his radiating enthusiasm by remaining cold and stern. She begins to see how her worst enemy transforms into her old friend, and to that, she begins to feel a fire in her veins.

Blank and Viola who witnessed the procedure stood frozen. Even the spectating prophet covers her mouth in shock when she sees that the Imporian had bestowed the gatekeeper the magneta scarf. Freaking out upon the spread of the champion's scarf, Ophelia begins to pant heavily. Her enemies – the gatekeepers of Imporia, have stressed her out far too long. She catches herself shuddering and breathing loudly. Filled with pressure, the prophet dreadfully slips towards the lower levels of the arena.

"I regret what I've done! I should've just stayed asleep when I had the chance! I spoke without knowing anything and after facing the harsh reality of this void, I can't dare to envision you getting hurt! Especially by me! I can't lose you! Not again, Zyra! I can't afford wasting our time like this!" Volt compassionately says, mustering a couple of tears.

The gatekeeper tenses up and readily aims her sword at the Imporian. "I don't think we're done here." she assertively calls out. Volt's cheery face quickly shifts into a surprised expression. "I've already told you a thousand times – *I'm not done with you.*" Zyra declares, this time with a sneer written over her rosy face.

The Imporian fears for his life. Had saving her from the Astra's red expiration been a grave mistake? Volt was fully aware of the damage he caused her, yet believes he could compensate by gifting her the true scarf – a real symbol of strong bonds. He hesitantly backs up only for Zyra to stomp forward. She relentlessly marches against him, causing the Imporian to grasp the idea of escaping. The gatekeeper drops her blade and collapses onto his torso. Zyra falls onto Volt with a tender hug.

The duo gracefully embrace each other. Volt heartily chuckles upon realizing that his friend had forgiven him of his brash actions. Zyra softly giggles at the fact that her friend had pardoned her of her villainous methods at saving him. The two fall onto the clay ground with tears of joy.

Reunited at last.

As Zyra firmly squeezes her savior, the fangs coming out of Volt's scarf begins to glow brightly. Perhaps it was the combination of bestowing a magenta flap while squeezing the source, but Zyra begins to physically transform a bit. Just like how Thevenin grew fangs and fin-ears, Zyra simply had her own subtle variation of change. Although she was not monster-like, motifs could be detected from afar.

To this, Zyra cockily unscarfs the red cloth underneath her newly rewarded magenta flap. She then confidently tosses it to Blank. "You want to fight for it?" Zyra comically snaps.

The prophet manages to reach the bottom floor of the arena. She stammers in disbelief, making inaudible noises. Ophelia emotionlessly glares at Volt in disbelief. "You...!" Ophelia stutters to herself with an uneasy flow of air. "You were never supposed to give it to her...!" she unsteadily whispers.

The appearance of the prophet draws everyone's attention.

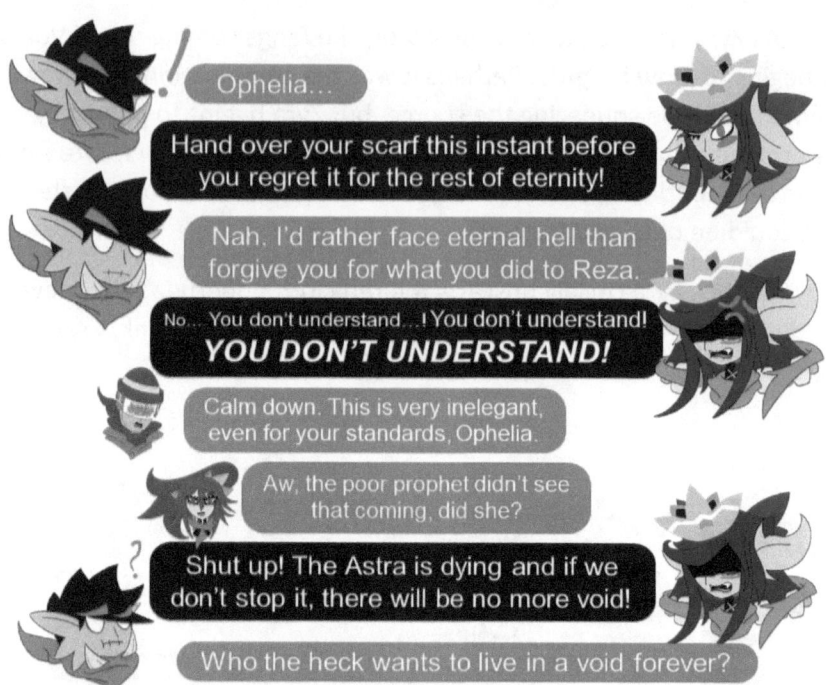

As Ophelia's tantrum breaches unsettling concerns, Viola tilts her head. "You're not really a prophet, are you?" Viola questions, startling Ophelia. "It's all in your head too, isn't it?" she adds as Ophelia's heart-rate races.

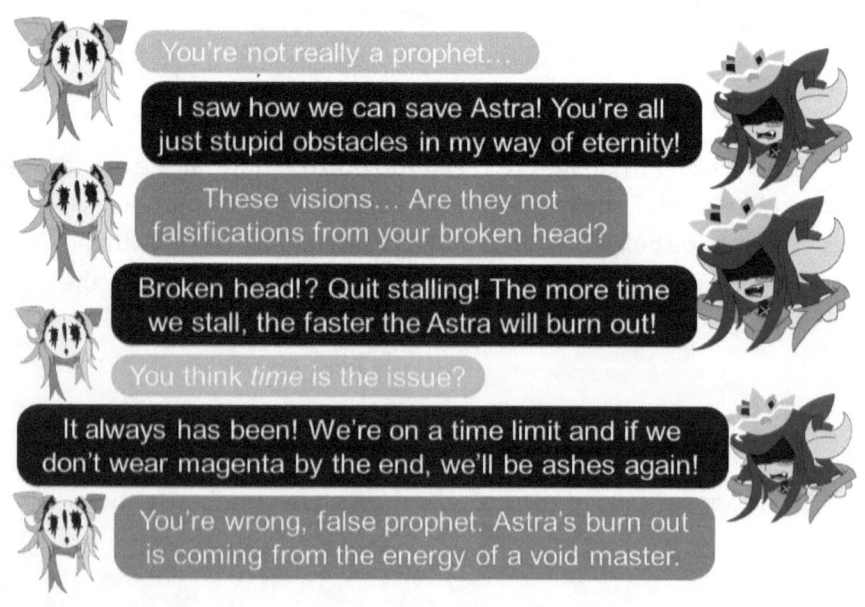

The duo that happily held each other were observing the electrifying argument, forgetting their own conflicts for a mere moment. "Why are you such a pain in the ass!? Do you not care about life!?" Ophelia dreadfully grunts as Volt grimly nudges in, "Clearly, you don't either." Zyra then jokingly adds, "Fun fact, Blank likes making people miserable too."

Viola then takes a step closer to Ophelia. "You are definitely wrong about your assumptions, *false prophet*. The Astra doesn't dwindle over time." the maiden speaks up. Grabbing everyone's attention.

The maiden with the spotlight aims her direction at Zyra. "The Astra does not fold over time because time is already frozen in the void. Has the evidence not been apparent?" Viola speaks. This revelation ultimately strikes Ophelia's core – of course time doesn't flow in the void... Yet, would wishing for the avoidance of the Astra's expiration render useful to her?

"You should've known by now that it is the void master that is in charge of the Astra's conditions." Viola firmly states. "In fact, it looks like the void master has been lying to you about its true intentions." Viola adds with a bit of sorrow in her tone.

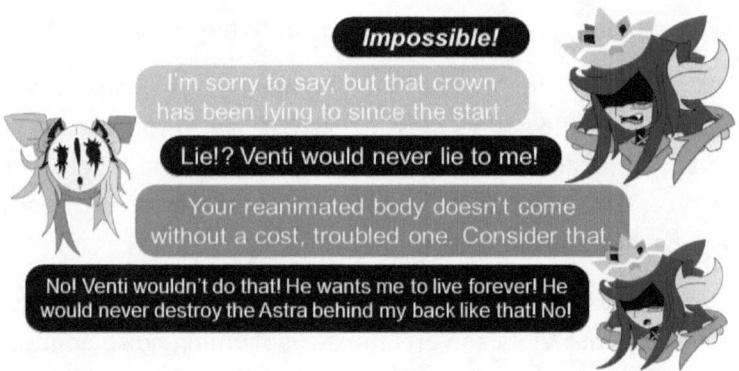

"It's been dormant since you've wakened up from your eternal slumber." Viola states. "How do we know it's not using you? Hasn't it manipulated you to desperately desire winning the election?" Viola continues to question.

In shock, Volt and Zyra give each other a wild glance. During their heated conversation, Ophelia's crown begins to rumble. "There's only one way to make sure that this 'Venti' doesn't ruin the election for anyone." Viola declares as she slowly puts her hands onto her mask.

"Wait, Viola! I don't think that'll be necessary!" Blank nervously spouts. Before he could get his message across, it was too late for Viola to hear his plea. Viola takes off her mask only to reveal a dark hole. In unison, everyone gazes at the vantablack face in awe. In the fraction of a second, Viola's face flashes a blinding light.

Without warning, the ground violently shakes, extreme winds were pulling the group into Viola and an intense vacuuming noise pounded everyone's eardrums. The true void begins — Viola's face had transformed into a literal black hole, seeping in the water-colored patches all over Void Imporia while obliterating the arena.

Chapter XVII:

Hellish Deadlines

Sins require punishment...

The arena shakes and crumbles violently. Refusing to fall into the black hole, Zyra digs her sword onto the ground. Both the gatekeeper and Imporian hang on for their survival. Blank rapidly strikes his pin-arms onto the rippled grounds, copying the duo's movements. Ophelia weakly grounds herself and clenches the floor with her remaining broken claws.

The gravitational pull that Viola had produced was far too great for mere pavements to stop them. Bit by bit, everyone slowly slides closer towards the hectic hole. Blank catches sight of the perilous situation. After all, the duo slides faster than anyone else in the arena. He cycles between pins as a method to walk without getting carried away by the intense winds.

Once he reaches the duo, he helps them resist the consuming vacuum. "Plate face!?" Volt shouts out, feeling the pull get weaker. The three huddle up together, enforcing more weight. Blank mutters in strain as he struggles to hold Volt and Zyra. Blank plants his pin arms into the ground and begins to transform his hands into tree roots. This secures an invincible foundation against the violent black hole.

The arena itself was breaking apart in chunks. The weak walls were torn away from its concrete structures. Even the cracks on the floor were stretching apart. Large chunks of the arena rip apart from its original position and fly above the trio.

Holding her ground, Ophelia screeches, "Stop this madness, Venti!" The struggling prophet then glances at Viola's fixed body. Seeing the maiden's red ribbon tied around her neck disheartens the prophet. Deep down, Ophelia knows that she cannot do yank the scarf off of Viola's neck thanks to the betrayal rule. Her crown continues to vibrate violently as Ophelia's expression drops from hopelessness to pure disturbance.

She faintly hears vibrations that ring in her head – as if the crown continues to communicate to her. The voice ruffles and claims that stopping Viola's tormenting suction would require impossible sacrifices and potentially, self-destruction. This impales Ophelia's mind – had Viola been telling the truth? Does the void master truly control the flow of the Astra?

Out of desperation, the false prophet remembers an object she had been hiding up her literal sleeves. Ophelia pulls out a compilation of stitched scarfs. With her talonless hand, she holds the bundle of scarves victoriously. "F-Fine! I'll just have to repaint you all!" Ophelia roars. With just enough colors for everyone, the ill-minded false prophet grows bitter confidence on stopping those around her. Primarily, she glares at Viola.

The false prophet then unlatches herself and flies towards Viola. "Zoriadia! We can't let her harm Viola!" Blank cries out. "I think we have other problems...!" the gatekeeper replies, attempting to stand her ground. "I think plate face is right!" Volt spouts as he lets go of his hold of Zyra. Volt begins to fly outwards only for Zyra to catch one of his loose flaps.

Turbulent suction roars across the entire void.

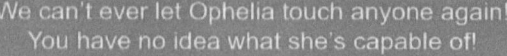 Dummy! What do you think you're doing!?

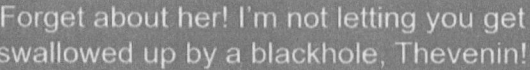 We can't ever let Ophelia touch anyone again! You have no idea what she's capable of!

Forget about her! I'm not letting you get swallowed up by a blackhole, Thevenin!

Dammit, Zoraidia! We can't afford to lose Viola! She's our only hope in imprisoning that bitch!

Sorry to break the news to you, but if you're that concerned about Ophelia, then we can unscarf her after she stops the blackhole!

No, you don't understand! Ophelia was never the problem, it was the void master controlling her!

 You mean the crown on her head?

Exactly! Doesn't matter what happens to Ophelia, it's the crown that needs to be locked up in that blackhole!

 ...Zyra! This is our only chance in ending all of this madness! Let me do this! I can knock her right in!

 You're an absolute dumbass if you think I'm letting go!

 Then I will!

"Hell no you won't—" Zyra spouts before feeling absolutely light. Heartlessly, Blank lets go of the velvet scarfers as their bodies fly towards the black hole. Without any warning, they hurdle and crash into Ophelia's frail body. In what felt like slow motion, Zyra, Volt, and Ophelia were all surprised that they collided into one another.

Due to how intense the pull was, the victim crashing victims were flung directly inside of Viola's consuming black hole. "Viola! Stop this now! The void master, Ophelia – even the velvet scarfers! They're all gone!" Blank

180

bellows, straining his voice. "Seal up your mask!" Blank cries out again with urgency.

Regardless of Blank's commands, Viola continues to violently intake everything around the void. If anything, hearing Blank's demand intensified the suction.

Suddenly, all types of particles, broken structures, and water-colored patches were coming straight at her. Viola's pure strength single-handedly begins to consume the entire island of Void Imporia.

"What are you doing!? Stop this now!" Blank screams at the top of his lungs. His veins begin to mark on his neck as he exerts all of his forces onto holding himself onto the ground. "Viola!" Blank cries out once more as he struggles to hold himself together.

Inside the true void was a pitch-black subspace. Only spurs of water-colored patches flew into the endless abyss. These bypassing colors were able to emit light near the exhausted prophet and helpless gatekeepers. These articles of photons eventually evaporated, making the embodiment of color fade into darkness.

Everything inside the maiden's head begins to evaporate into nothingness. Miraculously, the compilation of stitched scarves somehow were stuck on the border of Viola's entry hole. It appears as if some of the stitches were entangled at the entrance. Could this be the reason why Viola could not stop herself?

Volt opens his eyes to see that his elbow has been stuck to the open loop of the Zyra's sword. On the other end, Zyra is tightly grappling the sharp edge of the blade while using her free-hand to hang onto the large string of stitched cloth. "Thevenin!" Zyra screeches as he begins to regain consciousness. "C'mon! We need to get out of here!" the gatekeeper says as she is drenched in sweat.

He hesitantly nods as the heat of the true void quickly overwhelms him. As he begins to climb towards Zyra's dangling position, he suddenly feels tugging his foot. Ophelia had been weakly holding onto to his foot – she wasn't knocked out.

For a brief moment, Volt glares at her to quickly notice that the Ophelia he's been facing doesn't resemble anything he was used to seeing.

Did the heat get to him or is there something more going on?

Before anyone could speak, Ophelia's crown was floating away from the trio. It continues to rumble until it eerily spurts out tons of bloody veins...

"Ophelia..." the crown's voice echoes creepily. "V-Venti...!" Ophelia, or the former Ophelia-looking lady fearfully spouts. "There is no more hiding..." the crown continues to speak as it continues to transform into an unknown monstrosity.

"Y-Yes! It's time to break these gatekeepers apart once and for all!" Ophelia excitingly states. As the crown continues to build up a new form, Ophelia's body equally subtracts itself out of existence. "W-What are you d-doing, Venti?" Ophelia suddenly pleas in terror.

Volt and Zyra gawk at the evaporating prophet. "We are going to live forever, r-right?" Ophelia's damaged voice box pronounces. "You've been a wonderful pawn…" the ominous voice spoke. "A-Aren't we in this together…?" Ophelia questions with doubt.

"Indeed… I've only ever requested uninterrupted power from your impish soul…" Venti spoke. "Y-Yeah! Just hop on my head again! We can stop those two together and then—" – "Silence." Venti interrupts as its vibrating words evaporate Ophelia into multiple particles. The stomachs of the observing gatekeepers flipped upon seeing Ophelia dissipate on command. These particles did not evaporate into nothingness, however. Like a magnet, they were collected by the crown.

"Ophelia!" Volt bellows in angst.

This continues to mold the crown's evolving shape into something more horrendous. Seeing the prophet's life being snatched at an instant dropped the gatekeepers' hearts. Both Volt and Zyra witness this with wide eyes. What was once a pesky prophet who persistently bothered the duo by wedging herself in their cracks no longer ceased to exist — her physical energy horrifyingly shapes the upcoming nightmare.

"You…!" Volt timorously shudders. He could easily stay angry at all of Ophelia's actions, yet seeing her suffer the same fate as any innocent Imporian boils Volt's spirit. With the revelation of the void master and its mechanics, Volt slowly begins to sympathize for the bubbly prophet.

"It was you that destroyed Reza, didn't you!?" Volt cries out into the dark void. "You were the one that caused all of those damn vibrations in the sky, didn't you!? Answer me, you freak!" Volt's voice passionately grows angrier.

As the crown amalgamates into its final form, Volt's courageous anger shuts down into pure disgust. Indescribable fear strikes him and Zyra upon laying their innocent eyes at this… 'thing.'

"Champions…" Venti spoke as it's defining figure continues to shape itself. "…What on god's green earth are you…?" Volt fearfully cries out.

The enormous behemoth releases an echoing snicker.

"I simply couldn't keep my eyes off of you..."

Eternal Seeking Ventriloquist Zombiteer

"Finally..." Venti, the parasitic crown echoes. "There is no escaping the true void, competitors..." the monstrosity continues to speak.

Gawking in trepidation, the floating gatekeepers scan their vision at the infinitely towering crown. Zyra clenches the sowed ribbons tightly as her trembling muscles focus on pulling herself towards the exit. Particles and broken structures continue to vomit through the black hole's entrance. Their matter dissipates in a matter of seconds, encouraging the hanging gatekeeper to escape. If she is still in one piece, perhaps there is a way out...

"You... You're the one that created the hatchening!?" Volt panics. His unsteady expression indicated obvious fear, yet his words stood firm. Could this creature have initiated all of his suffering?

"Since I am no longer limited by Astra in this realm... I will reclaim what is rightfully mine..." the crown's voice echoes. Without warning, bright dots surround Volt's body. With these bright lights surrounding Volt's body, small transparent lasers begin to glow as if they were strings connected to the crown's atrocious talons. "Return to me..." Venti adds as it's one disdained red-eye glares at Volt. "Why are you doing this!?" Volt hopelessly screams out.

"Perish." Venti's voice vibrates across the dark void.

In the flash of a second, thousands of sharp red harpoons impale the champion's body. The strike obliterated Volt to the point where he could not even release sound. At the top of her lungs, Zyra screeches the name of her fallen comrade.

Absolutely sickened.

Zyra could not realize that her rekindled friend has been punctured in incomprehensible ways. Between the mixture of all the heat, the sheer disgust in Venti's true form, and the annihilation of her comrade, she could no longer control her brave guise. Horror drenches into her soul as tears cannot fathom emotional liberty. What worth is there in challenging such an unstoppable force?

"Extraction..." Venti commands as the impaled darts sucks the magenta colors off of Volt's dangling body. With the now string-attached dead body's scarf returning to its original grey colors, Zyra hopelessly swings her blade to cut off the bloody streams. "The champion's stain is mine..." Venti announces as Zyra's attacks do not even inflict any sort of damage towards the crown. "Now it's your turn." Venti echoes as it directs its focus onto Zyra.

More of the shining dots begin to cover Zyra's quivering body. Momentarily, small strings of transparent lasers strike out of her figure. "Rest in permanence." Venti's eerie voice bellows as it begins to peel its talons out of Volt's punctured body. Zyra's heartbeat races faster than ever as she braces herself for the thousand-needled impact.

Upon effortlessly pulling off its pins from Volt, the harpoons yanking get stuck. Venti continues to retract the stuck spears until suddenly, it no longer moved. A blinding electrical explosion burns the harpoons into nothingness. "Reboot complete!" a voice distantly alerted.

After the vicious flash, Zyra opens her eyes to see that Volt's body was no more – instead, it was the figure of her long-lost friend, Thevenin. Severely damaged but oddly in one piece, Zyra latches onto the floating body tightly. "Thevenin!" she gasps in utter surprise. Unconscious, Thevenin rests safely in Zyra's embrace.

The matter that Venti had pulled off was the resting soul of a relentless warrior – brightly shining in front of the gatekeepers was an electrical amalgamation of Sympl. "...It is time for this unit to release Volt." Sympl starkly declares.

Impossible... Heartbreak murdered you.

Bold of you to assume a small metallic shell could store all of my voltage.

Fair game indeed. This is where you perish.

Is that...? Sympl? Is that you?

"Please protect the last scarf, Zyra. Master has done more than enough for all of us. We cannot lose the election now." Sympl suggests as its plasmatic figure blows the gatekeepers towards the direction of the black hole's exit.

"Over my dead body!" Venti screeches as it darts a relentless number of harpoons towards the escaping gatekeepers. Zyra sees the rushing spears jolting towards her neck. In an instance, Sympl's amalgamation zaps the spears out of existence preventing any possible injuries from occurring.

"Zyra, use this opportunity to seal us up!" the plasmatic Sympl demands towards the alerted Zyra.

"You won't get the chance!" Venti screeches out once more as it reaches at Zyra with its gigantic clawed hand. Once again, Sympl's plasmatic body grapples the incoming attack and empoweringly shoves Venti away. The overwhelming power of Sympl's plasma induces anger towards the disfigured Venti.

Hence, Sympl wraps the gatekeepers in non-charged cables. "Now, go and be happy!" Sympl commands, this time it aggressively launching the gatekeepers through the hole, allowing them to escape.

As the gatekeepers were forced out of the darkest void, Zyra looks behind to see Sympl ready to tackle the beast. Zooming out in style, the duo plunge out of Viola's head.

"You god damn fool..." Venti's hostile voice continues to vibrate around the void. "You know what'll happen to us if a mere Imporian wins this damned election..." Venti scourges. "I'd rather shut down knowing my host is happy than let you become the king of the voids." Sympl replies.

You will never understand what it's like to have someone's back.

And you'll never understand what it feels like to be ahead of someone.

Did you forget that we'll trapped here forever once this void as been sealed? Just as perfectly planned...

 As long as I'm here to guard that gate away from you, you'll never attain the eternity you truly desire.

The two monstrous titans clash with all of their might. Each blow they exchanged causes devastating vibrations that will never be experienced by any other living being.

Will the titans clash until the end of time?

Viola's vacuuming weakens slightly, making Blank tug the gatekeepers out of the black hole. "Put the damn mask on already!" Blank commandingly yells. The maiden hears his desperate request. Viola then struggles to move her arm, but once she holds out her mask, the vacuum instantly places it over her face. This seals the water-colored patches, the destroyed bits of the arena, and more importantly, Ophelia's presence.

Finale—II:
Last Astral Ribbon

Farwell...

With a lid on her face, Viola adjusts her mask carefully to ensure that it wouldn't accidentally fall off or produce anymore succulent effects. Ironically, being in Void-Imporia was a welcoming feeling for the gatekeepers. With the black hole being capped, Blank gasps for air as he instantly rushes over to the gatekeepers.

Still shaking at the events that had just occurred, Zyra triumphantly exhales. The crown that had been gnawing down the Astra was sealed up and assumed to be defeated. At the very least, it now is sealed under Viola's mask as it continues to battle the soul of Sympl. Zyra looks at her hands as they still violently quiver.

The masked leader reaches the gatekeepers – "Did you finally stop Ophelia and her damn crown?" Blank frantically asks. "...What the actual hell just happened...?" Zyra asks as she finds the evaporating Imporian peacefully resting.

That's right – Thevenin, the Imporian that once had fin-ears, crisp lips, huge pupils and yellow skin has reverted to her old friend. *Thevenin.* The unconscious friend has a faint smile written over his face as colorful particles begin to leave his body. His evaporation trickles at an extremely slow pace.

"Thevenin!" Zyra cries out, bending over to the unconscious Imporian. "Hey, this isn't a time to disappear on me…!" she gloomily says, shaking his corpse in an attempt to wake him up. "Blank! Do something!" Zyra angrily demands as the masked man helplessly watches.

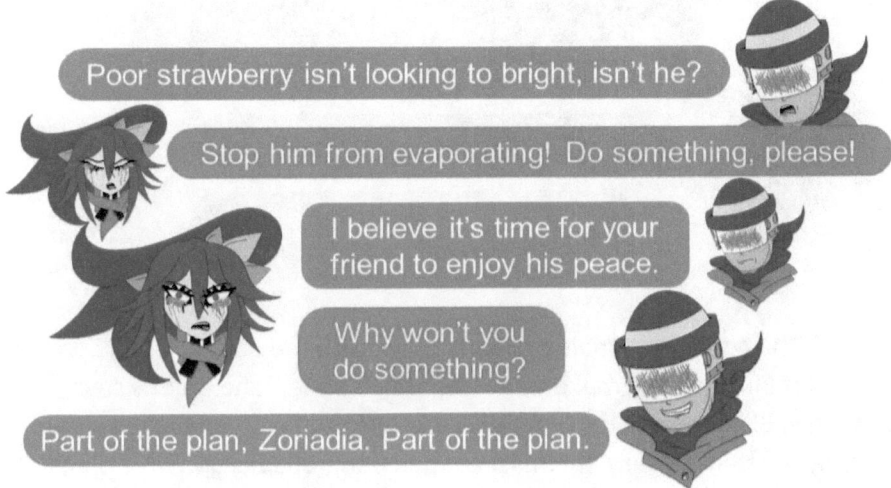

While Zyra struggles to save Thevenin, Viola approaches Blank. "Mister Blank… Zoriadia! Are you two okay?" she asks in dwelling concern. Instantaneously, the maiden finds Thevenin peacefully laying on the ground, slowly fizzingly away. She releases a muffled gasp, in shock of what her ink-painted eyes saw.

Deep inside of Viola, she knew that Zyra and Thevenin had served an important role in stopping the void masters. As a result, she earnestly wishes to accommodate them into Aphotic. That way, she wouldn't have to see them suffer a terrible fate. Guilty, Viola begins to burst aloud.

I'm so sorry! I think I vacuumed for too long!

It's all good, Viola. We're on the verge of victory now.

It's all good!? How could you easily say that!?

Ophelia and the void master is gone. The Astra will no longer dissipate, and the champion's scarf is gone. Besides your scarf, this is the best result we could've possibly asked for.

B-Best result!? Everyone's dead!

Oh, Zoriadia! There may be one way to save your friend!

The concerned maiden lightly plays with the dangling scarf on her neck. "I think I need to make up for what I've done." she quietly says. Suddenly, Blank begins to clap his hands. "Not so fast, Viola. I never said that my mission is over." the masked man eerily speaks up. Viola blankly stares at Blank's bleeding face-plate, "What do you mean, Mister Blank?" she asks curiously.

"Young missy, we both knew you were crucial to the plan..." Blank applauds. As the masked man's clapping comes to an end, he begins to release an annoyed sigh. "But there's only one way to confirm that all void masters are truly gone." Blank says, snickering. The maiden tilts her head in amusement. "What do you mean by that?" Viola curiously questions.

"Begone, Viola." Blank coldly says. The pained mask-wearer rapidly transforms his bleeding arms into pins and slices the maiden in half. Before Zyra's very own eyes, the yarn maiden was split into two. Viola's ragdoll body hits the ground with her mask falling off. Unlike the last time she removed it, there were no violent black holes, just spurs of cotton spilling out of the hole. The maiden's mask rolls like a coin around until it eventually falls flat. Despite being separated from the scarf, Viola's lifeless carcass does not evaporate.

Speechless, Zyra flinches in agony. She tries to comprehend how swiftly Blank took out Viola – After all, didn't she just hint that she could stop Thevenin from melting? The gatekeeper does not hesitate to draw her blade. In a vigorous rage, she slams her blade against Blank, who simply uses one of his bleeding pins to stop her from cutting him.

"You monster! You! You're ruining everything!" Zyra belligerently roars. "Under no circumstance will I forgive myself for allowing another champion to be crowned." Blank cold-heartedly replies. With no possible way to save her friend from his slow evaporation, Zyra is pushed back by Blank. "Now with that headache asides, we can confirm that you're the last one standing." He smirks.

The empty-hearted masked man tallies another red mark on his faceplate, making his face-plate absolutely red. "You're... You're a cruel, pathetic man!" she tears up. "Cheer up, fruitcake. It's time to celebrate the end." Blank meticulously announces. "...Right after I get rid of you." he eerily adds as he embraces his blood-red gaze at Zyra. The gatekeeper raises her blade, ready to strike at the twisted masked man.

The two engage in a duel where they recklessly swing their pointy weapons at each other. "After your death... There will finally be undisturbed peace!" Blank growls. Zyra desperately tries to keep up with her swift movements as she tries to jab for an opening but only finds herself blocking more often than striking at him. Grasping the gravity of the situation, Zyra's adrenaline kicks further in.

As if the two were exchanging blows, their fighting grew more vigorous and riskier. Zyra's rage peaks as Blank's confidence grows larger. In one of his strikes, Blank successfully slashes his pin arms across Zyra's torso, causing her to scream in pain. To this searing pain, Zyra lashes out another attack that tears Blank's weak shoulder. He too yells out of sharp pain.

"Stop this! Stop!" Zyra cries out as she powerfully swings her blade and knocks off Blank's mask clean. Instantly he lays over and continues to shy his face away from the struggling gatekeeper. Out of exhaustion, Zyra slowly hauls herself to her knees. "Why... Why are you so miserable!?" Zyra screeches as she continues to destructively pant. "The election stole everything I've ever had... And I'm not letting you do the same mistake again!" Blank replies as he sluggishly goes for the final blow.

What felt like a lifeless moment, Zyra's eyes widen out of shock. She felt cold chills riddle down her spine. She could not comprehend what she had just witnessed. Zyra's blade had impaled Blank through his torso. Perhaps it was out of pure reaction or out of instinctive autonomy to defend herself one last time. Blank's shutters in the mighty sharp pain.

A part of Zyra urges her to apologize as another part makes her stay silent. The flinching leader begins to tear up and struggles to breathe. He transforms and places is arm over the wound. "Don't do this..." he whispers. She hesitates. Zyra could see Blank's pained eyes as he tries his toughest to guise his sorrow. Clearly seeing the face of the masked man for the first time definitely prevented her from robbing him of his scarf.

There was something very human about his exhausted expression. It triggers Zyra to ease up and regret all of her movements. But in his last resort, Blank ambushes the distracted Zyra by hastily transforming his arm. Right before he could grasp her scarf, Zyra swiftly swings her blade and robs Blank of his scarf.

"W-What have you done..." Blank stutters once he understands that this is indeed his end. Seeing Zyra's triumphant stance freezes his core. He shivers slowly and tucks down his steamy face. "Zoriadia..." Blank whispers agonizingly. In the heat of the moment, Blank hallucinates his previous election run.

Did history really repeat itself?

"You promised that you'd use another chance at happiness to free us all…" Blank words to himself, catching Zyra off-guard. "You lied… You're a filthy traitor… None of us wouldn't be here right now if you delivered your end of the promise, Zoriadia." he sorrily mutters.

His enraged words brew utter anger. "I pledged my undying trust to you…" Blank grits. As the heat from his body continues to stir up, his realty distorts with his sweat. Blank tries to sit with himself – he observes his quivering hands disappear in front of his face.

Blank rises-up one last time. Unlike the floored Imporian, Blank's evaporation accelerates at a fast pace. Lasting excruciating seconds. "I hate you…" he snarls to himself.

In the flash of a second, Blank extends his evaporating pin arms and strikes at Zyra's neck one last time. Reactively, Zyra swings her blade at Blank's pin, blocking off his movement one last time. From this point and onwards, the evaporation process Blank experienced made it physically impossible for him to grapple anything anymore.

In defeat, Blank glances at his disappearing arms. He silently stares at his phasing arms, then glares at Zyra with his repressive expression. Subtly nodding to himself, he glares at Zyra. "You're going to regret winning for the rest eternity…" he unsettlingly hints. Slowly coming to terms with his evaporation, Zyra gawks at what she has done. Blank then dissipates out of Void Imporia.

And with that, the Astra begins to rumble.

With every single red-scarfer out of the void, the Astra's red appendage doesn't curl up into a petal. It falls from the colorless skies. Zyra sees this event from the distance as she grows uneasy. The massive ribbon falls like a feather. Yet, once it makes a touch down to the void's cold floors, an unsettling vibration explosively bursts throughout the entire island.

In its end, the sound of a loud bell rips chunks of Void Imporia apart, as if the island had been hit with a blinding supernova, identical to the one that started the entire void. Earth-shattering earthquakes breaks the island's tectonic plates, creating a hazardous terrain for the remaining champions. Tiny bursts of intense fire erupt through the various cracks around the island. These enraging flames consumed nearby resting swords, glamorous crystal shards, swampy grass, and fertile grounds.

After feeling the world-ending vibration explode, she quickly scurries to her friend who is still taking forever to evaporate. Seeing Thevenin emit colorful partials awed her. His faint smile and the spectrum of beautiful colors gave his resting body a gentle glint. Peculiarly, she notices how Thevenin's scarf's color was a glowing grey. How come a grey scarf of all colors resisted for so long? The gatekeeper breaks away from this peaceful distraction and desperately scavenges for a solution to stop him from melting.

"You were the only one to reach out your hand for me during the inferno... That day, you gave me another chance at this cruel world, now it's my turn to return the favor!" Zyra spouts upon ripping her own scarf into two pieces and resting the woven cloth over his neck.

Placing half of the magical cloth doesn't necessarily change his pace of evaporation. "Thev! Please hang in there!" she dreadfully calls out. The gatekeeper then places the other half over her neck. "Look! Now both of us are wearing the stupid bib! It's like what you promised, remember?" she begs. With no response from the unconscious Imporian, Zyra slams her fists on his chest. "Please, wake up!" her outcry gets lost given that her friend could no longer hear her pleading voice.

Zyra closes her eyes and sobs over the silence of her truest friend. "Please don't go..." she whispers one last time.

The overwhelming heat, the shaky grounds, and the shocking lash-out the Astra had produced continued to crack the void into utter darkness. Zyra attempts to open her eyes, but her vision fails her as the void became pitch black. Or could she simply not open her own eyes again?

She feels herself blinking, yet simply could not detect a difference when she was awake or not. Did the explosive Astra rob her of her own life? Is she undergoing a different phenomenon? Was this the forewarned ending that Blank and Ophelia had alerted the gatekeeper about? In these crippling moments, Zyra begins to be deprived of all of her senses...

And just like that, Void Imporia was no more.

Epilogue:
Enter Another Chance at Happiness?

Total darkness — as if Zyra could not open her eyes again. After the void is consumed in total darkness, absolutely nothing remains. Suddenly, a spotlight shines on Zyra's crouching body. Another spotlight reveals a fancy gate with open doors. Confused, she gently stands up and hears a voice in her head.

"Welcome to the final gate, Champion. Due to all of your efforts in the void, you have been elected for another chance at happiness. What you desire most in your heart will be manifested once you walk through the gate. Be warned – there is no limit to what you wish to have as long as you know what you want."

The final gate? Is this what the champion of the election is sent to? Zyra ponders in tremor. She patiently observes the silent void and begins to accept the voice's conversation.

Who... Who are you?

"Who or what I am does not play an important role; I only exist to serve. Even if that means reshaping the entire universe to fulfill your desires, it shall be granted for as you are the last of your kind."

I've been warned about your methods.

"Correct, Champion. There is absolutely no holding back. That is an expected reward for you and your trials. You must understand that the scarf you wear is a symbol of relentlessness, overcoming impossible odds, and most importantly – tragedy. After walking through the final gate, you will be placed in a position where you no longer need to feel the emptiness in your heart."

Where is that spotlight coming from?

"Interesting question. Is that really what you want to know?"

Actually, no. Can you luminate this void?
I don't want you hiding any doors from me.

"Very clever of you, Champion. Your analytical nature plays an enormous role in your success in winning the election. However, rest assure. This empty space is just that. There are no boundaries, yet no matter how far you travel away from the final gate, you'll never reach anything else. This, Champion, is the end of the election."

The spotlights brighten as it reveals one empty void. In front of Zyra stood the fancy gate. Nothing surrounds her as the honest voice had forewarned. She looks all around her to see absolutely nothing else. Like an astronaut in a space without stars, she felt hollow.

What if I refuse to walk through the gate?

"Unfortunately, you have nowhere else to go. However, you may stay here for as long as you want and truly think about what you desire. This is not any choice you are taking though. What brings you joy will quite literally determine the next world."

...The next world?

"The world you remember was crafted in the vision of the last champion. That is at least how all worlds are generated." Imporia? The island of Imporia was perceived as a thought of a previous champion? Still unsure, Zyra continues to speech.

May I ask about the records of the last champion?

"Once again, that information renders uselessness since it has no value for your heart; it will not influence you in any way, shape, or form."

Am I truly the only one left...?

"This election has concluded itself with a grand total of **two** champions. This isn't the first time this has happened before, however."

Thevenin! That means my scarf worked! Where is he? Wasn't he with me just now?

"When multiple champions win, they are not allowed to walk through the same final gate together. Each champion receives their own reward. As a result, you will not get to meet the other champion here. Also, it is improbable that you will ever encounter the same version of the other champion in your next world." Hearing this detail frightens Zyra. Does this confirm that she will traverse into obscurity?

"If your heart desires to reunite with past friends, chances are that they will align with the version that exists in your head. In other words, certain details that exist now may not translate to their authentic form... This is a place only designated for you and you alone. The manifestation of your true desires will handle the rest."

This statement causes the analytical champion to focus on the voice's words. Does this imply that she herself will be all that can be known to exist? Will other versions of her past be manifested into falsified malformations? What if she could go back in time to keep their forms as authentic as possible? Would doing this equate to risking an unchangeable future? What about an alternative universe where she can live out her wildest fantasies and never worry about life's painful laws?

With stricken harmful information, her head begins to race at infinite speeds. "I can feel the burden this choice has narrowed you with. Do not fear, champion. Your head may pump an unlimited amount of ideas on where to go, but your heart will be the one choosing." Scared, Zyra speaks up again.

 How do I know when I'm ready to walk through the gate?

"Champion, you've been through hell and back. I'm confident you'll be prepared to take the leap of happiness when you are comfortable." In silence, Zyra continues to gather her thoughts. Is this voice stating truths? If so, why with this transparency? Did Zyra really deserve to unearth these many questions? The gatekeeper exhales heavily.

What really happens to me when I walk through the gate?

"No need to doubt the final gate. You will finally fill your heart with happiness. Think about it as if there were another adventure that awaits you — except, not traumatizing at all! Get excited because this means you are quite literally a few steps away from exploring your wildest dreams."

 ...What if my heart is wrong?

"Champion, there's only one way of finding out."

The champion of Void Imporia's tragic election faces the final gate — her chance at happiness awaits her. "Please take your beautiful time, champion." The inner machination of the Astra's voice spoke to her.

What truly resides inside of Zyra's heart? What are the consequences she's projecting? Where does this gate lead? How will the world handle her heart's truest desires? As for all of these questions resides one true answer...

Only time will tell.

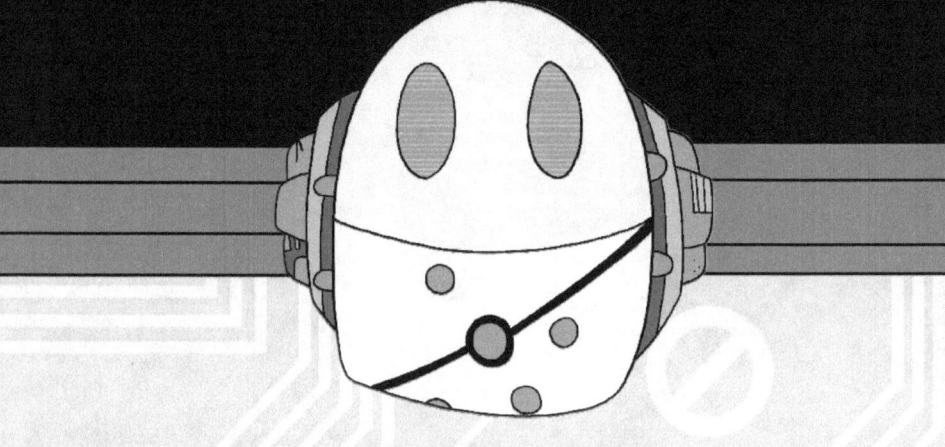

"Congratulations! You found my secret private diary of noteworthy events that since I woke up in this void! This is only meant for the eyes of Volt!

Message to Master Volt:

I know you're kinda slow since your brain is basically turned-off, but no worries! If you ever wanted to review something, look at this as an appendix. Be warned though! Not everything is meant to be seen all at once. Try to break it down or review it after we've reached a checkpoint!

Sympl's Datalog

According to what I was able to log during our adventure, I've gathered definitions of odd terms I've never seen before! How exciting! Here is my detailed log of information I was able to download during our blank hike!

Imporia – Apparently, it was an island where people used to live festively. For some reason or another, my host really misses that place even though I have no clue what life was like up there.

Void Imporia – Currently, this is what is left of the island. It's deprived of its aforementioned festivity; everything lacks pigment and feels colorless. Very rarely can you see water-colored patches scattered in this empty lot. Personally, I can't relate to my partner's anxiety, but this place truly is home; it's all I've ever known... At least, this is all I know.

Volt (or was it *Thevenin*?) – This dude thinks I'm a vampire. Clearly, I'm a dog. Bark-Bark. See? No matter. It doesn't matter what I am. I needed to store my voltage into something that can sustain me, otherwise, I'd shut down and who knows what would happen then! He tends to ask a lot of questions, but I don't know how to answer most of them. Who created me? Where did I come from? Was a born to shut down? Most of the time I just stayed silent. To make things less harsh on his back, I decided to nickname him Volt. Maybe then we can move with the right foot forward.

S-y-m-p-l – A robot that – hey wait, that's me! Previously, my internal program only referenced me as "This Unit." This was overwritten by Volt when he spelled and registered my name as "Sympl." I'm capable of a large number of things. What type of things? Oh, y'know! Mountain climbing, flipping pancakes, defensive war tactics, data logging, triggering a nuclear winter, and even preventing the entire—huh? My program states I can't do most of these? Hmm... Perhaps we shall develop my skills as we adventure?

The Hatchening – According to various dialogues I've recorded between my host and that pesky Ophelia, the hatchening was the main event that destroyed the entire island and gave birth to Void Imporia. What I am still trying to figure out is why Ophelia assumes that the hatchening gave birth to a monster. Volt is not a monster! She does not have enough evidence to prove that Volt is one! He's a very juicy, noble man who wants to help me maintain my battery levels!

Gatekeepers – During our time in the relatively gray sinkhole, Volt explained that he was a part of a team of gatekeepers – people who spend their lives on the verge of preventing disasters. I was unable to see this in action since Volt was really shy! He ended up running away from pretty much everyone we met.

Tactical Cable Arms – These are my means of defense. While I've been grappling to Volt this entire time, I still have a couple of loose wires I can use to protect or serve our bundling blows!

Warning: I can't guarantee the safety of our targets when I use it on them.

Ugly, brain-dead witch – Zombified creepy lady that wears a shiny crown. At first, I was really glad she helped us escape from the relatively gray sinkhole. Then, the more I started gathering data, I realized that something wasn't right. She's very insidious in her wording and frankly, unpredictable. She's also really ugly, no way Volt would fall for her charms! At least, I hope. She definitely has something up her sleeves...

The Election – Ophelia basically said that the election is the competitive process of holding onto your scarf until you are the last one standing. She says that the champion of the election will be rewarded another chance at happiness. She must've been very confident in Volt since she kept calling him champion – his name is clearly Volt.

Another Chance at Happiness – Is this a video game? Well, according to recorded accounts, once you win another chance at happiness, you may have one unrestricted wish granted. The unrestrictive part is something to take precaution with. Hmm... what would I wish for if I won the election...?

Astra – A beautiful compilation of ribbons in the sky! Way prettier than Ophelia. Seriously, why did Ophelia think Volt was talking about her?

Fake-keepers – Also known as "the doofs," these are a group of people who wear the same armor as Volt. Albeit, for some reason they're different colors and are not actually real gatekeepers. Perhaps the hatchening did something to their clothing? All they did was attack us and that's not nice.

Aphotic – A legion of goons who have teamed up to stop anyone from winning the election. They're conducted by their leader – Mister Blank. For a dwindling group of masked people, they sure really want to make people miserable. I bet it's because Blank wants to win the election and use his wish to give everyone who helped him a delicious cookie!

Mister Blank – This dude is a big meanie. Like, a really big meanie! One thing to note is how he has this odd ability to transform his bleeding hands into pins as a means of offense. This void truly is horrendous with all of these unknown variables in the air. I do wonder though; did he get that ability from sheer will or has he perhaps found out a way to exploit the void's energy somehow? Oh! And those tally marks on his faceplate... What do they signify? I have so many questions! My biggest question is how can he even see his environment with a faceplate that thick!

Heartful Reza – Anxious fake-keeper who saved our butt. I think we owe her a big thank you! Although her teammates are nasty at their core... Of the times we met, she really proves herself to be someone that wants to protect people! I do not understand her motivations, but she definitely acts like a gatekeeper if I've ever seen one. If we meet her again, I want Volt to take the time and thank her for her services!

Zyra – Apparently, a real gatekeeper and an old friend of Volt. I wouldn't dare call her that though! She is intentionally trying to hurt Volt and that's just no good! Why would a gatekeeper of all people want to hurt Volt? Is she under the influence of Aphotic? When we spoke, she firmly believes that Volt is the reason why survivors in the void are evaporating... What the heck! How can you conclude that? Regardless of whatever she thinks, it's also important to note that she analyzes situations quickly. Perhaps she speaks the truth or maybe is severely misunderstood... Nah, she's crazy-crazy!

Astral Vibration – Once the Astra officially curls up its appendage into a petal, the entire void suffers an unspeakable vibration that paralyzes the air we breathe. We have no idea what is controlling this... Is this what Ophelia meant when she said "Only time will tell?" Is time really the factor that controls it?

Twin-tied Astra – An eerie cloth-covered star in the sky that dictates the colors of the scarves. It took a while to understand this, but once one of its appendages folds up into a petal, the color of that appendage no longer has the ability to protect from violently evaporating. All of the appendages seem to be curling up into a petal over time. However, the magenta ribbon never displays any signs of moving... How strange. Maybe if we did win the election, we could stop this somehow? Then again, that would imply the evaporation of all life besides ourselves... This is a very concerning predicament. What would a noble gatekeeper do?

Heartbreak – This is a serious threat! If we can't unscarf that monster, we are completely doomed! Truthfully, is unscarfing even an option? It's super strong and has a ton of resistance in its blood! The best way to tackle such a monster is to hit her at her core! Even if we can't unscarf her, we must find a way to make it possible! Oh, and watch out if she stares at you too long! She can paralyze you with fear...

Unburdened Volt – Volt, if you're ever reviewing my data log, I just want to express gratitude for letting me use your body in order to continue surviving! I knew I could count on you since we met! That's why I'll still be there in your most desperate hour! I may not be on your physical back, but I'll be rebooting myself in your spirit – literally! I just hope you can hear me next time I detect an error...

Lost child – From what I felt, this child's aura is somewhat familiar. Data states that it shares an identical form of another being we've encountered, but how? We were able to confirm that by sharing our scarf, the child would be obedient and stay in the sinkhole, right? I hope he doesn't go anywhere too far...

Darkest Void Vortex-Point – While I didn't get a chance to properly download this object, I was able to complete my reboot inside of its mask. The darkest void is a realm independent of the Astra and its rules, so I could finally complete my true form thanks to her warm invitation.

Venti the Ventriloquist Zombiteer – Ah yes, it all comes back to me... I hid my true form into a robotic shell in hopes of stopping a void master like Venti from corrupting the Astra. Although, thanks to my host's skills and bonds, I was able to download his talents and copy everyone's battle-data to confidently defend the void from Venti.

Very Outrageous Light Terrestrial – Nurtured and flourished from the relentless body of my host, I was able to reserve the host's original form as a token of my appreciation. With downloaded skills of a gatekeeper, Venti shall never be released into Void Imporia ever again! Perhaps I shouldn't attempt to reboot when error fruits are in my host's blood!

I am confident you were able to seal us up inside of the darkest void...

But neither of us expected it to get darker..."

Thank you for your time!

Please consider following the author for more updates on future installments! Contact information at the first page of this book!

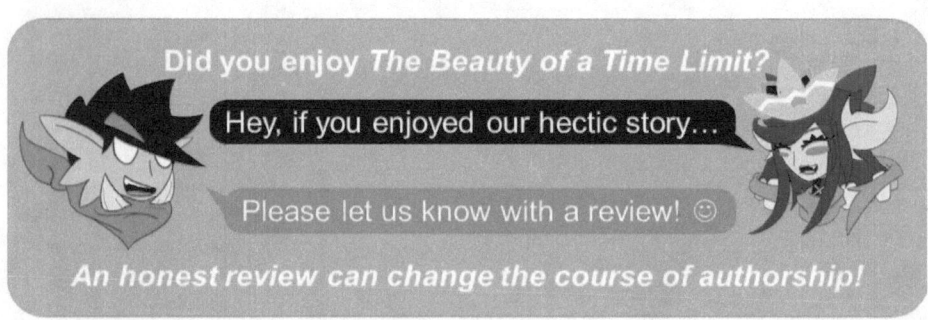

Next installment:
Another Chance at Happiness

Secret Password: VioLeka4evAR

Edwardivan Labarca-Torres is an engineer from Puerto Rico who spends his free time drafting stories, musical compositions, and even programs video games too! He's crazy over the idea of how limitless robotics can be and loves to give his readers deep-lore to think about.